This one is for my parents, who endured hours of
storytelling while I was growing up

Thank you for encouraging me to keep allowing
my imagination to run wild

The Wood Will Swallow You Whole

Published by Reading Nook Publishing

Published 2025

ISBN: 979-8-9878657-4-3

THE WOOD

WILL SWALLOW

YOU WHOLE

TABLE OF CONTENTS

ALL THE LAND YOU OWN
(AN ALZHEIMER'S ANALOGY)

You own a plot of land. On this plot of land there is a pond. In this pond lives a school of fish, a whole host of frogs, and an underwater treasure. A Great Heron visits the pond once a day to scoop up a fish, yet the number never dwindles.

One day, as you walk your land you notice a rip in the ground. It isn't that some machine has come through and tilled up the soil. It's more of a gaping wound that has not been sewn back together with sutures. This split makes you sad. It reminds you that life is fragile and even the earth beneath your feet is not immune to the violence of existence.

You follow the laceration and discover that it leads directly to the pond. The gouge disappears well below the water line, yet none of the water splashes over onto this ground. It's as if someone has placed a sheet of glass between the water and the dirt to hold it in place.

Curiosity takes hold and you return to your house to find a pick-axe and shovel. But as you walk you find yourself getting turned around. The common path you are used to walking every day becomes muddled in your head. It's like someone is rearranging thoughts in your brain to purposefully confuse you.

You stop.

You take a deep breath.

You allow your thoughts to coalesce into remembrance and then you continue your journey.

As you wander you look at all the land you have tilled and into which you have dug. There are pieces of ground you avoid because they remind you of something horrible and destructive. A shiver convulses your body, and your mouth runs dry.

How long have you been walking?

You don't ever recall it taking this long to travel from the pond to your house.

In the distance you see the structure you are striving for, and a sense of relief falls over you. It isn't until this moment you realize your heart has been beating fast in your chest.

Although the house is within your sight you sit to take a rest.

You listen to the sounds of nature.

It is soothing.

You recall fishing in a lake when you were a child; your father next to you; a million gnats buzzing around your head.

But now you have aged, and you can feel the cold settle into your bones and aches come and go without so much as an invitation.

You can't recall what you were going to the house for, but hunger hits you like a brick wall. If you don't eat something soon you know you will feel faint and perhaps even pass out as your blood sugar plummets. So, you pick yourself up off the ground and continue your journey to the house.

A patch of unfamiliar ground rises in front of you, and you furrow your brow trying to remember the last time you came this way on your land.

You question if you've ever approached the house from this particular angle before, but you cannot recall.

At least you can see the house from here, so you know you will be able to reach your destination.

Finally, after what feels like ages, your hand touches the familiar chill of the knob of the front door. You step inside, but immediately sense something is wrong. Although you cannot remember exactly how long you have lived on this land by yourself, you know it has been quite some time.

There are picture frames lining the walls of the entryway, smiling faces you seem to know watching you walk toward the kitchen. They are vaguely familiar, but the names elude you.

Now that you are in the house you have lost track of the task you originally intended to accomplish. Instead of worrying about it, you decide to make yourself a sandwich, but when you search for a butter knife you discover that everything has been rearranged in the drawers, which makes no sense, since you live here alone, and no one ever comes to visit.

Anger takes hold and you fling drawers open, throwing them to the ground, watching utensils and pens and rubber bands and papers crash to the floor in a tumult of sound that makes you cover your ears in self-preservation.

You open the fridge and stand in front of its artificial light, wolfing down lunch meat and cheese until the dryness in your throat demands resolution as a choking feeling almost overwhelms you. And you rummage through the cabinets but are unable to find a single glass to fill.

The rage builds inside once again as you wonder exactly who in hell could have moved your items around.

As the fury subsides, you walk to the sink, dip your head toward the running faucet, and drink deeply until your throat is no longer scratchy.

This act reminds you of your original intent for coming up to the house and you grab a pickaxe and a shovel and head back outside.

Upon your return to the pond, you notice that the gash has

deepened, and yet still none of the water has leaked backwards into the culvert. You imagine that if you could somehow allow the water to pass through to the dry earth, everything will be alright.

You put your hand against the invisible barrier between water and dirt and feel the pressure there.

It is almost unbearable.

So, you begin to work the ground, creating more space for the water to rush into, but no matter how much room you create, the water holds its shape and refuses to spill backwards and wet the earth.

As you investigate this strange anomaly you notice a small wooden box nestled in a tangle of underwater weeds and rocks.

It looks old and warped, worn away from years of neglect.

You remove your shoes and socks and roll up your pant legs and wade into the pond. Fish scurry away, leaving bubble trails in their wake. Frogs hop from rock to rock, croaking in disapproval at the disturbance.

The water gets deeper and deeper until you realize your chest is under the surface. You feel around with your toes until they graze the top of the box.

Without hesitation you dive, looking for the exact spot your foot landed a moment before.

There is no air in your lungs. It feels as though you have forgotten the mechanics of holding your breath and you fear that you might drown.

But the box persists.

As do you.

Panic begins to overcome you, but still, you struggle with the box.

Finally, your finger touches a latch and the lid opens. You need to see what treasure lies within, even if it is your last act. As the box reveals its contents, you hear a melody. Something you haven't heard in years, possibly decades.

Pictures float out of the box, and as they pass by and float to the surface, you grab some of them.

And you know the faces in the photos.

They beckon for you to follow them and you obey.

The sensation of flowing water tugs at your clothing, and you realize that the invisible dam has burst open, and the pond is expanding to heal the rip.

As you emerge from the water you realize you do in fact remember how to breathe and you inhale a lung full of air, grasping the photos tight in your fist.

And the melody persists, reminding you of everything you have ever forgotten.

Your house swims into focus and you recall where everything should be, and is, and you begin to cry.

Clarity rushes in and you hold tight to the memories.

An impending sense of déjà vu overwhelms you and as you, soaking wet, trudge back to your home you pray that if you are cursed to repeat the same day over again, you still remember how to breathe.

VICTORY LAP

The sound of the other cars was blurred to a monotonous hum as he rounded the final curve of the track and could see the finish line ahead.

Checking his periphery, he noticed the number 67 car attempting to nudge him toward the wall.

A voice crackled in his ear, "Watch it. Steady. Don't let him take you. Five seconds and you've got this."

"Copy." Sweat trickled down Macron's forehead, getting lost in his helmet liner before it could affect his vision.

Four seconds.

He hazarded a glance to his left again, noting the position of the nose of 67 and then peeked to the right to see how close to the wall he was. There was still enough room to outmaneuver his opponent. He allowed himself a smile.

Three seconds.

A sudden screeching sound filled the air, followed by a hard crunch.

Two seconds.

67 was no longer beside him. Something had happened, but there was no time to ask pit. He could see the flag, the official readying to wave it.

One second.

Taking a deep breath, Macron felt the elation run through his body. It was electric.

He crossed the finish line, saw the official wave the flag, and checked to see if there would need to be video replay to determine a winner. No other car was near him. The serotonin hit him, and he felt like he was flying. This was his first victory, in only his twelfth race.

Macron looked around, figuring that whatever had caused the wreck on the last straightaway had taken out any racers who had been trying to pass him at the end.

It was time for his victory lap. He shifted and slowed the car, pumping his fist against the top of his roll cage.

It took him another few seconds to realize there was no voice in his ear. No exuberant yells or excited curses infiltrating coms.

"Pit? What happened behind me?" Static.

His lap began to take on an ominous feel. What *had* happened to the other racers, 67 and everyone else.

"Pit? Does anyone need assistance?" Static.

Macron rounded the far curve and looked to the distant side of the track, but he didn't see a crash. There were no ambulances, no tow trucks, no cars.

"Pit?"

Get him out. Now! The voice sounded distant. Not so much in his headset, but…somewhere else.

He tried to reach his crew one last time. "What the hell is going on? Where is everyone?"

Did he say something? The distant voice again.

Impossible, came a reply, another voice that sounded even further away.

Panic hit Macron like a stone. He could hear people, but not see them. Did the crash send a car into the stands? Could he hear yelling from somewhere off track?

He hit his brakes, smelling the smoke and burnt rubber from his exhausted tires.

Reaching down he tried to remove his 5-point harness. It was stuck, jammed tight for some reason.

Trying to control his breathing, he put the car into a low gear and rolled into his stall.

It was empty. No one was there.

Dear Jesus, his helmet shattered.

"Hello?" he yelled, hitting the side of his helmet, understanding finally that there must be something wrong with his coms.

He yanked at his harness again, but still there was no give. Slamming his hands against the steering wheel he noticed he left behind a dark, slick substance.

"Oil? From where?" he asked himself, raising his hands in front of him, seeing the same substance on his gloves.

Finally, he looked down and saw the liquid slowly oozing from his lower abdomen. There was a bright flash of light and he thought, *Oh shit, a car exploded!*

He heard the same distant voice echo his own thoughts.

Then the panic returned with a horrible ferocity. Something was wrong. He couldn't breathe and his vision was blurring. A slow heat rose from his core and he knew he needed to get out of the car before he overheated and passed out.

"Where the hell is everybody?" he yelled as his vision dimmed further, allowing him only a slit to see the world around him.

He kicked his legs in a desperate attempt to jostle his harness loose, but instantly a sharp pain sent lightning throughout his entire body. He screamed in agony.

And then his vision failed him. The pain remained. He was going to die in his car.

He took a slow, shaky breath and tried to open his eyes one more time. It was blurry, but he thought he saw a whole crowd of people around him and he felt a strange tugging under his armpits.

The voices returned and sounded a bit closer. "I don't care if you have to break his leg to get him out of there! This car is going to go up any second and I'd rather him never race again..."

All sound went away.

All light went away.

The last thought Macron had, as he felt tears slide down his face was, *I don't think I won.*

HOMESTEAD

Charlene was making herself a breakfast of eggs, toast and bacon when she felt the growl of the diesel engines heading down her long driveway. She sensed it before she heard it, because her ears weren't working as well as they did before the blight. But she recognized the approach of motorcycles instantly. And if experience had taught her anything about motorcycles arriving at her homestead, it was to be prepared for whatever might be coming.

Post-blight America had done a number on millions of folks, her included. The disease that ushered in a new world had affected everyone differently. Most commonly people's hearing dimmed, and heart rates were a bit more erratic. But it wasn't uncommon to run across someone whose teeth fell out for no apparent reason, or whose hair came away in chunks. There were even documented cases of leprosy-like symptoms where the nerves were damaged enough to create a lack of pain sensation, allowing people to lose fingers or toes without realizing it.

But Charlene didn't mind any of that. She suffered from a bit of hearing loss and there were days when she stayed in bed because her bones felt very brittle. But, she had her purpose. Purpose that had not existed before the blight.

In her former life Charlene was a designer, anything from shelving units to whole houses. There were countless magazine articles dedicated to her work. It wasn't an obscure life, but it wasn't as glamorous as some might surmise. Yet she made do and thoroughly enjoyed coming up with new ways to re-create the same old things.

The engines cutting off in the drive brought Charlene back from her reverie. Moments later she heard the footsteps of at least four people, maybe as many as six, walking up the wooden stairs to the front porch. There was a hard rap on the door that shook the hinges ever so slightly, and Charlene took the pan off the stove so she didn't burn her eggs or bacon, wiped her hands on the towel hanging at her waist, and walked to the door.

There were five separate locks for security, and she undid each one slowly and methodically. The reason for this was two-fold: first, she could gauge the impatience of those waiting for her to answer her door, and second, she could overhear even low conversation and that allowed her to determine what type of group she might be dealing with. As the last lock snapped open, she stood tall, sighed deep, and opened the door wide.

"Welcome weary travelers," was all she got out before the big man, who was obviously in charge, pushed her and sent her sprawling. Snickers arose from his merry band and no one made an attempt to help her back to her feet.

She stood back up, brushed the dust off her clothing, and said to the back of the leader's head, "No need to be rude. I was simply welcoming you to my humble abode."

He scoffed. "Humble? Lady, this house is nicer than 90% of the shitholes we've passed."

Charlene simply smiled and moved back toward the kitchen, talking over her shoulder.

"What brings you fellas here today? Passing through? Looking to settle somewhere?" She smiled warmly at the band of four. They didn't return the sentiment.

"We're travelers. No home could sate us like the call of the open road." The leader turned to Charlene and grinned a humorless, greasy smile. Most of his teeth were rotten, a few had fallen out along the way.

"Although," he continued, raising his eyebrows as he looked around the living space.

Charlene interrupted. "Oh, no no. I didn't mean my place. There are plenty of farmhouses in this area that have been abandoned. Probably just need a little tidying up to make them livable again."

The man stepped menacingly toward Charlene, but she held her ground, and her smile.

"My dear lady," the leader said, trying to put honey in his tone and failing. "What's to stop us from killing you and taking your land? I mean, there are four of us," he gestured around at the others, "And only one little ol' you."

If he had hoped for her to beg him not to perpetrate such an atrocity, he was sorely disappointed. His face fell when he realized his intimidation tactics were ineffectual. Then he shrugged his shoulders and began picking up random items, keeping one eye on Charlene at all times.

She watched the leader for a good long while and finally replied, "I mean, that's all fine and well if you want to tend the garden and clean the house and fix all the issues this ol' girl has, but something tells me you're not the homesteader type."

He stopped and turned fully toward Charlene. Taking two steps forward he saw Charlene glancing down and to the left. Finally, he had gotten through to her. He now held the power.

"And what type of person do I look like to you?" he asked with a sneer.

"The type who thinks he can intimidate anyone into doing whatever he wants them to do. And I imagine it usually works. I mean, you sure are a big fella. You look to be about six-and-a-half feet tall,

320 pounds? Am I in the ballpark?" Charlene sized him up while she spoke, and then scoffed.

The leader took one more step forward, realizing he hadn't in fact frightened her at all. Now he was inches from her face and she could smell the rot emanating from his mouth. Not to be outdone, his body smelled as ripe as a garbage pit. But she didn't flinch.

"Maybe," he began, running his tongue over his remaining teeth, his gums bleeding from its light touch, "Just maybe I let my men all take turns with you." He looked her up and down. "I mean, you are a bit old for my tastes, but desperate times, as they say."

This drew a few lascivious chuckles from his compadres. And the leader saw that Charlene was smiling and shaking her head.

"You see, this is the problem," Charlene said, patting the man on the upper arm. "Once again you have failed to grasp the situation, so let me spell it out for you. If you kill me, there will be no more food grown here. This will no longer be a safe haven for people where they can fill their bellies and wash off the road under hot water."

She glanced around and noticed that the mention of hot water had actually gotten their attention.

"And if any of you attempt to harm me in any way, I will end both that man and myself. I *will* not be humiliated. And I may be in my 70s, but that doesn't mean I don't care a spit about my own life."

Charlene folded her hands in front of her waist and looked from man to man to see if they were truly catching her drift. It appeared that they were, so she clapped her hands once, watching them flinch from the sound.

"Well then, it seems as though you gentlemen could do with a bit of bathing. But before you do there are a few rules. First, if you have anything to trade for the privilege of staying and bathing and eating at my homestead, that will be discussed shortly. Second, the bar of soap you use to bathe with is yours to keep. It should last you at least a few washes before running out. Third, do not go into the forest. As the old tellers of tales used to say, there be beasties there."

One of the other men finally spoke up. "I think I can handle a couple of coyotes and bunny rabbits."

Charlene stared at him for a long time. Long enough for him to shift uncomfortably from foot to foot and look away. She shrugged her shoulders and said, "Two showers upstairs, one tub down the hall here. The water heater is holding up nicely and it is tankless. Enjoy your showers and baths. Take all the time you need. Lunch will be at noon on the dot. If you are not at the table then, don't expect me to make you something special."

The men all looked to the leader, and he gave a small, nearly imperceptible nod. They all rushed off to clean themselves up, but he remained behind for a minute longer.

Charlene turned and scooped her eggs and bacon onto the plate that already held her toast and made her way to the dining room table. He followed her every move and sat down in a chair opposite her. She could see him licking his lips and smiled.

"I need to eat my breakfast, if you don't mind."

The man nodded to her as if to say, 'go ahead'.

"What's your name, big fella?"

"Cal," he replied quietly. Most of his attention was still on the food on her plate.

"Cal, I'm Charlene. It's nice to make your acquaintance," she replied before picking up a forkful of food and dumping it onto the toast.

She watched his reaction closely as she crunched down on the toast slowly. He was a big man, but he definitely looked a little malnourished. She held out her second piece of toast to him and he grabbed it from her, chomping it down in three bites.

"Water," he growled through the crumbs in his mouth.

Charlene shot him a disappointed look. "The world may have ended as we know it, but manners still count. I'd say they count even more now than ever."

Cal stared right back at her as he started to cough. "Please," he replied, through gritted teeth.

As Charlene stood, she patted his hand. "See? That wasn't so scary, was it?" She moved off to fulfill his request and heard the sudden rush of water through the pipes.

The sound startled Cal and he physically jumped, almost falling out of his seat.

"Oh, don't mind that, dearie. Old farmhouse, old pipes. Nothing is quiet around here." She returned with the glass, and he drank it dry as quickly as he had devoured the toast.

The sound of more water rushing through the pipes signaled a second shower being turned on, and then the pipes running from the back of the house started up and a moment later a blood curdling scream filled the air and the lights dimmed.

Cal was on his feet in an instant, staring into the fearful face of his host. He moved past her toward the back of the house, Charlene following close on his heels.

"Oh no. Oh no. Oh no." She kept repeating the words with a hand over her mouth.

They reached the bathroom and noticed that much of the water that was in the bath had sloshed onto the floor. Cal moved up to the edge of the bath, but Charlene reached out and pulled him back quickly. He turned on her, open hand stretched out above his head, ready to smack her across the face.

Charlene didn't even flinch. Instead, she pointed to an exposed wire that dangled into the tub, letting him know silently that if he had tried anything he would have been electrocuted himself.

"I'm so sorry about your friend," Charlene said with tears in her eyes. "I didn't think to mention the wire." She glanced at the man in the tub, who was not moving. Her eyes focused on his neck, no pulse.

"And why the hell not?" Cal screamed in her face.

"Because if he had simply come in here and gotten in the bath instead of snooping around, that wire never would have fallen. Unfortunately, no one has traded me anything that would be useful in helping me fix the exposed wire, so I tuck it away as best I can. And the only way it could have fallen is if he was doing something he ought not to be doing."

The sound of footsteps could be heard from upstairs and a few seconds later one of the other men came running into the bathroom, stark naked. Charlene didn't seem to notice, but Cal shielded his eyes.

"Dammit Bo, put that thing away. Nobody needs to see that."

"Sorry boss," Bo panted. "I heard a scream and didn't know what—" He finally looked past them and into the tub where his friend lay still, small tendrils of smoke curling up into the air. "Oh Jesus," he whispered reverently.

Charlene moved past the two men brusquely. "Now, if you'll excuse me, I need to go flip the breaker for this room so I can restore the wire to its rightful place." She turned back to them and pointed an accusatory finger in their faces. "And maybe this will teach you to not go snooping in someone else's house without permission."

She moved off, leaving the two friends to stare at each other in utter disbelief. A few moments later the lights in the room went dark. About a minute after that Charlene entered the bathroom with a flashlight and dutifully threaded the wire back where it was above the bathtub and wiped the exposed end off with a towel to dry it.

"There," she muttered and went to turn the breaker back on, adding, "Either put some clothes on or go back to your shower, young man. I personally don't need to see that shriveled thing dangling between your legs any longer."

Bo, still in shock, replied, "Yes ma'am," and moved off to return to his shower, leaving Cal temporarily alone in the bathroom with the dead body.

After a moment or two more he made his decision and pulled his friend from the tub, hoisting him over his shoulder. He tromped back to the dining room and heard the click of the breaker box. A moment later Charlene walked around the corner.

"You got a place I can bury him?" There was still menace in Cal's voice, but it was subdued.

Charlene shook her head. "No place that wouldn't spoil the food growin' in my ground. Sorry."

She moved past Cal and sat down to finish her breakfast. "There is a shed out back you could store him in until you leave. But I'm afraid I'm going to have to insist he go with you when you continue your journey."

Without another word, Cal stalked out the front door, slamming it shut behind him.

Charlene calmly finished her food and then cleared the table.

She heard the water being turned off upstairs and waited for all three men to return to the dining area. The two showered men, Bo and the as-of-yet unidentified third man, walked down the stairs in their stale, smelling clothes and Charlene shook her head at them. "This won't do. If you go down the hall and take your first left you will enter the laundry room. There are robes you can put on while you wash your filthy clothes. I will let Cal know when he comes back in the house."

The third guy looked at Charlene, confused. "Where did Cal go?"

"He went to put your friend in the shed for safekeeping until you all leave."

The un-named man rolled his eyes. "What did Mitch do this time?"

Bo swallowed loudly. "Ummm…" he began.

Charlene stepped toward the man and put a reassuring hand on his wrist. "Dear, your friend was electrocuted, I'm sorry to say. It has only happened one other time, but it was my own foolishness that caused it. I understand if you want to throttle me right now, but I can assure you it was an honest mistake. I am terribly sorry."

The man's face contorted with rage, and he stepped into Charlene, knocking her back a foot, nearly sending her sprawling to the hardwood floors again. Bo reached out a hand to restrain him. "Trev, don't. Let's at least get a couple good meals and some clean clothes out of her before we *reward* her for her incompetence."

Trev remained in his threatening pose for a few seconds longer before backing off and nodding his head.

Charlene adjusted her clothing and said, "Down the hall. First door on the left. I'll let Cal know about it too. Maybe you can all throw your clothes into one load. I may have water, but eventually something's got to give."

Bo and Trev walked away, leaving Charlene alone once again. The reprieve didn't last long, because a moment later Cal walked back through the front door. He glared at her, but she could see the very real grief cross his face for his lost friend.

He walked up to her and through gritted teeth said, "Anything I should know about upstairs that might kill me while I'm trying to take a shower?"

She calmly shook her head and said, "If you would like your clothes washed one of your buddies can follow you upstairs and put it in the laundry for you." Without waiting for him to respond she yelled, "Hey Bo! You want to bring Cal one of those robes and then get his clothes to wash while he showers?"

Bo trudged back out into the dining room carrying a robe and silently followed Cal up the stairs and out of sight.

Charlene went into the kitchen to do the dishes and caught a glimpse of Trev heading toward the front door.

"Mind what I said about the woods," she called out to him. "It would be terrible for anyone else to get hurt."

"Shut up," he muttered, and walked out.

When Charlene finished with the dishes, she turned around to find Bo staring at her. He had a hungry look in his eyes. She sighed and gestured for him to sit down at the table. After a moment's deliberation he acquiesced. Lowering herself into the chair next to him she said, "I would like to tell you a little story. Is that all right?"

The danger remained in his eyes, but he nodded tersely.

"Very well," she began as the water flowed through the pipes once again. "I used to be a designer. I designed cabinets, pantries, housing layouts, most anything that could be designed architecturally, I had a hand in it. Now, I can tell you are mad at me because of your friend Mitch. And I'm sure me telling you that I was a designer isn't putting your mind at ease any, because you're probably telling yourself that I should have known better. This is true. I'm not denying it.

"But, as you are well aware, the world has altered slightly since the blight, so items are more difficult to come by. What you could go down to the hardware store to buy, you can't even beg off a friend on a good day anymore. That is if you still have friends. Which you do."

"I thought you wanted to tell me a story," Bo growled at her.

"I'm getting to that part," Charlene responded sweetly, patting his hand.

"Anyhow, a short while ago a couple came to stay with me. The woman was very pregnant, like ready to pop that baby out into this world pregnant. Myself, if I was still of childbearing age, I wouldn't want to bring a newborn into this hellscape. But she was filled with optimism. Hope. Even when she went into labor that night and I was unable to save her life she continued to smile and repeatedly encouraged her husband to not worry and to take care of their newborn.

"The father was distraught. I've never seen a man break down and cry like that man did. But she simply kept on saying, 'Sweetie, it's okay. You get to take care of our daughter. What an honor and privilege. I love you and am so proud of you.' There wasn't a bone in her body that was filled with regret or rage at the indifference death had for the pure of heart.

"She passed before she discovered she had given birth to a baby boy. But the man didn't have the heart to give the child a boy's name, so he named him after his mother. There is a young child out in this crazy world named Lily. And he, God willing, is alive and thriving with his father.

"Fortunately, I had the materials to build a coffin for the mother, and I was also able to help him bury the body a couple miles down the road. This was when I still had horses, of course. If I tried anything like that without them I would probably keel over and die from over-exertion before I got beyond the property line.

"The point is shit happens. Death is a part of life. It is inevitable. And I am truly sorry for your friend. But if you look at it from another perspective, maybe his departure at this point in his journey will save him from a lot of pain to come.

"There isn't a day goes by that I don't think of Lily and hope he is out there truly living his life. Maybe one day he and his father will stop by my little homestead, and we will get to have a reunion. Maybe it will be the same with you and your friends. But if you let that rage control you, you might as well be as dead as Mitch."

Charlene stared deep into Bo's eyes and saw the first sign of genuine emotion in them. She had gotten through to him in some capacity. At least she wanted to believe she had.

The water stopped flowing through the pipes and a minute later Cal came down the stairs wearing his borrowed robe. Instead of coming over to the table he moved around the room looking at different objects. It took him a moment before he realized someone was missing.

"Where's Trev?" he suddenly asked.

"Your friend said he needed some fresh air. Don't worry I warned him again about not going into the woods, so he will be fine. He's probably down in the garden eating some fruits and vegetables."

Cal's face darkened. "Shit! I can guarantee you he went into the woods. He's like a petulant child. Tell him no and he'll do it that much faster."

Both men rushed out the door yelling Trev's name, and Charlene slowly stood up and followed them outside, a look of concern on her face. She stayed on the porch and watched the two men race along the edge of the forest, trying to find their friend.

When he didn't reply to any of their calls Cal made as if to enter the trees and Charlene finally intervened. "Cal! If you set foot in there don't expect to see the open sky again. If Trev made the decision to ignore my warnings that was his decision to make. And if you even think about taking it out on me I will take you down in the process."

Cal stopped with a foot in the air and then stalked over to Charlene. "Did you just threaten me?"

Charlene stood up to her full height of five foot three and replied, "It's a warning. That's all."

They stared at each other intently for a long minute and then they heard Bo yelling for them. Rushing to where he stood outside the woods, Charlene peeked through the foliage and saw a body slumped against a tree. His head hung limp to one side, held on by a few random pieces of flesh. It looked as if some creature tried to rip off his head, but didn't quite succeed. She heard the gurgle of Bo's stomach followed by the sound of dry heaving.

Cal actually looked frightened but hid it as best he could.

Charlene looked at Bo and saw the shock glazing his eyes. Without hesitation he brushed past Cal, got on his motorcycle and rode off, the borrowed robe flapping behind him in the wind.

After what felt like an eternity, Cal turned back to the woods and seemed to be about to walk in to retrieve Trev, but Charlene gripped his arm tightly. "Unless you want to suffer the same fate as your friend there, I would suggest coming back to the house. I will make you some lunch and then you can be on your way."

She could feel the tension in his arm but held firm until it loosened, and he started the trek back to the house.

When they got inside Cal sat heavily in a chair at the table. Charlene made herself busy in the kitchen, putting together sandwiches. Cal remained silent until Charlene returned with the food. He pushed the plate away from himself and leaned forward, close to Charlene's face. Still he said nothing.

Charlene took a bite of her sandwich and gestured to the one she had made for Cal. "Please eat. You need some meat on your bones."

"What happened to your husband?" Cal suddenly asked.

Charlene smiled at the memory of her husband. "That is a tale indeed."

Cal leaned back and grabbed his plate, taking an enormous bite out of the sandwich.

"You see," Charlene began, "My dear Harold was the one who came up with the idea for this homestead. We had always lived here of course, but after the blight it became evident that people were going to need help. There was a lack of resources available to most people almost immediately. Not enough people planned for *the apocalypse*, as people referred to it all over the internet.

"So, Harold figured that if we had a waypoint along the path of people's travels, we could offer them food, a hot shower, and a safe place to sleep for a night or two before moving along. And it has been wonderful. We only started trading with people when we realized our resources would quickly run out and we would be left in much the same situation as so many others. If Harold had not insisted on the barter system we would have been done with this endeavor a year into all of this. But he always did have a good head on his shoulders."

Cal shifted in his seat and Charlene held up a hand.

"I know. I'm getting to the meat of the story, but I need you to understand the person he was. Have patience."

She stood up and moved toward the kitchen. "I could do with some milk. Would you like some milk, Cal?"

"Fine," Cal said.

Charlene grabbed two glasses and set them on the mobile butcher's block that sat between the kitchen and dining room.

"I freeze the milk. That's how I still have some left even though I'm sure you noticed I don't have a cow."

Cal stared daggers at her.

"Anyhow," Charlene continued, grabbing the milk from the fridge and heading back toward the butcher's block. "One day along came a group, not much unlike yours. They were brash and rude and angry and selfish, demanding things and pushing my sweet Harold around. And Harold being Harold took it all in stride.

"The morning the group was set to leave they tried to steal some of our equipment. Harold went to try and reason with them, but they shoved him to the ground… hard.”

Charlene stopped and took a breath to compose herself before continuing.

“I'm sure you've seen what the blight does to people, Cal. What it did to my husband was make his bones brittle. They weren't glass, it wasn't quite that bad. But too much pressure on any part of his body could shatter his bones.

“Harold hit the ground, and I heard a snap. He looked up at me with his kind eyes, pleading for help. I only got to be with my husband for another few seconds, because when he landed, a piece of his rib bone broke off and found its way directly into his heart. He was dead before the group had left the property.”

She took a deep, shuddering breath and a single tear trickled its way down her face. Cal remained stoic, in his seat.

“I said I had a purpose. And that purpose is to help those in need. I provide them with food, a hot shower, and a place to stay.”

She glared at Cal, and he noticed a shift in her demeanor immediately, but stayed seated.

Charlene continued, “But sometimes I'm reminded of my other purpose. I'm sure you're aware that people can have more than one purpose, right Cal?” She didn't wait for a response. “And that other purpose is to ensure that groups like yours don't get the opportunity to hurt the people you meet along the way.”

As she finished the sentence she opened a drawer in the butcher's block and pulled out a pistol, aiming it at Cal. Cal jumped up out of his chair, knocking it halfway across the room. An evil smile crossed his face, and he took a step towards Charlene. The only thing between him and Charlene was the butcher's block and she made sure it stayed that way.

“So, Cal, here is where we stand. An old woman who simply wants to help people against a man who wants to hurt them.”

"Put down the gun!" Cal snarled at her.

He moved one way to try and step around the butcher's block and Charlene matched the movement. He shifted the other way, and she followed suit. Cal was becoming very agitated, but Charlene remained calm.

"I truly believe that everyone deserves to eat. But I don't believe that everyone deserves to live."

She pushed the gun forward with resolve, her aim rocksteady. Cal watched her carefully.

"What do you want from me?" Cal asked, venom dripping from the question.

"Just look up every once in a while. See what's around you. See *who's* around you. You are so busy looking out for yourself that you forget there are others struggling just as much, if not more."

Cal watched as the resolve and energy seemed to drain out of her.

He nodded. "I can do that. Give me a chance."

Charlene still had the gun pointed at Cal, but he sensed that she was close to putting it down.

Charlene spoke softly. "I want to believe you. I really do."

Cal put his hands together in a pleading gesture. "Then believe me. I'm telling you the truth. My crew is gone. I'm on my own now. I don't have a choice but to rely on the kindness of others."

They looked at each other for a long time, nobody moving, nobody speaking. Charlene looked away for a moment and her arm fell slightly. Cal took advantage of that to fling the butcher's block aside and rush Charlene.

Cal didn't have time to register the shot that rang through the dining room before he collapsed in a heap on the floor. His breathing hitched as he stared at the floorboards, blood seeping out around him. Then he felt himself rolling over and he was suddenly staring at the ceiling. He couldn't register what he was seeing.

Charlene appeared above him and smiled kindly as he lay there dying. "I warned you. I told you to look up, but you refused."

She moved out of the way and then he saw it. The barrel of a shotgun stuck down through the ceiling. Smoke still trickled out of the business end.

Charlene watched the light fade out of his eyes and then pushed his body off the panel he had depressed when he moved forward to get at her. The panel slowly returned to its original position with a gentle click.

She stood there for a long time, her age catching up to her. She wasn't as spry and lively as she once was and she needed her heart to slow down before she could take care of the rest of it.

Finally, after what felt like an eternity she grabbed Cal's wrists and began dragging him toward the front door. "I'm pretty sure I mentioned I was a designer. All you had to do was look up, Cal, and you might still be here."

There was a wheelbarrow on the far side of the porch. She grabbed it, lowered it to the ground, and rolled Cal's body into it. Then she made her way towards the forest.

Once inside the forest, Charlene made a few turns she knew by heart and arrived at a makeshift graveyard. There were only a few graves, but after this night there would be a few more.

She dumped Cal's body on the ground and collapsed next to a wooden grave marker. On the marker was the name "Lily" and Charlene touched it with affection.

"I hope your boy is doing well out there. I hope he has your spirit and is helping those he can along the way. That he can bring a little heaven to this hell."

Eventually she stood up and made her way toward where Trev's body was. She picked up the metal knives shaped like claws and put them in the wheelbarrow. "I am thinking I need to sharpen you a little bit. Messy work this time. It was supposed to be a clean cut."

She looked down at Trev and tilted her head to one side in a mockery of his current condition. "I will be back for you young man, but you'll keep for now."

Charlene made her way back to the house and stared at the mess that used to be a part of Cal.

"Time to clean up and reset," she said to nobody.

And then she got to work.

THIS, MY SHADOW

Paranoia has been laughed out of serious conversation for as long as anyone can remember. Nobody is out to get anyone else. There is no purpose behind indulging someone who suffers from paranoid delusions. The answer is generally to place them under psychiatric care, whether that means they are admitted to a facility, or they are monitored closely by doctors to ensure their safety along with that of those around them. Paranoia can lead to hysteria, a concept that has been mislabeled since the earliest days of medicine. Unfortunately, if an idea crops up that has no easily available answer, it is either dismissed or demonized. Hysteria was demonized and labeled as only occurring within women. I understand what hysteria feels like, and I need it to be known that I would not wish this upon anyone ever.

All this to say that I understand the frustration that is involved with misappropriating ideas and concepts. I have been the butt end of many jokes and unwanted concerns for the last few months. This may be my own fault, because I was daft enough to tell a few people about my problem. There was a small space inside my head that felt the tiniest bit sane, where the paranoia hadn't reached yet, that spoke softly to me, telling me I could trust these others with my little secret. I don't listen to that voice any longer.

Instead of beating around the bush, I will speak plainly of the issue I have. Either I will be believed, or I won't. There hasn't seemed to be an in-between.

Frankly speaking, my shadow is trying to kill me. If this was an audio story, I would pause here so everyone could get out their scoffs and giggles and eye rolls. I am well aware of how this sounds. And if someone told me their shadow was trying to kill them, I would most likely react in a similar fashion. All I ask is that I am allowed to lay out what has happened to me recently and leave it up to each person to make their own determinations.

I feel like that isn't too much to ask.

In January of this last year, I sat at my desk in my study, my lantern burning low, the filaments crackling softly. There wasn't much light, but it was enough for me to cast a shadow upon the paper of my journal. I wasn't paying much attention to the shadow, since it had accompanied me my whole life and was as natural as breathing. However, as the light from the lantern guttered signaling the end of my supply of oil, I imagined I saw my shadow separate itself from my movements and set about its own mission. What its intent was I couldn't say, for I was flabbergasted by even the thought that my shadow could be its own entity.

Removing my spectacles and rubbing my eyes, I told myself that I was exhausted from my studies and was hallucinating. So, I put out the lantern, stashed my journal and pen in the drawer of the desk, and went about my bedtime ritual with about as much fervor as I employed when buttering bread in the morning. That is to say, not much.

Although I had nearly convinced myself that I had not witnessed what I had imagined, my mind returned time and again to the slight movement within the darkness that contradicted my own. It is difficult to truly explain what I thought I had seen, but I will attempt to do so to the best of my abilities.

I had finished a paragraph dealing with demonology and the influence of supernatural entities upon the physical realm and when I lifted my pen from the parchment my shadow scrawled one last word onto the page: INFINITE. Yet, when I looked at the paper in front of my eyes there was nothing to be seen. And when I focused back upon my shadow, the word had vanished. This is why my mind took the route of exhaustion as explanation. And I believed it at the time. I am still quite exhausted, but I no longer believe that was the cause of my vision.

Jumping to mid-March, I had only borne witness to two other instances where I thought I saw my shadow move of its own devices, but both times I had only caught the movement out of the corner of my eye. Once again, I had chalked it up to exhaustion and I vowed to enforce rest for myself in order to regain whatever equilibrium I must have lost during the first couple months of the year. No more occult studies, no more digging into the origins of the spiritual realm. At least, not for a couple months.

On March 25, in the year 1899, my opinions changed regarding the state of my mind. I had returned from the market after a rather embarrassing fall, wherein I spilt my fresh produce all across the road. The cause of my tripping was not immediately apparent, as the ground was flat and seemingly without obstacles.

I went to my bathroom cabinet and removed gauze and iodine to tend my elbow scrape. Returning to the kitchen, I set about the task of treating my wound and trying to remember where I had placed my kit to sew up the jacket sleeve that had torn during the incident. When I turned away from the table, the sun shone through the bay window, suddenly bright and intense. There against the far wall my shadow was cast in stark relief. Almost dark and sharp enough to imagine it as a portal instead of a ghost of mortal existence.

That is when my shadow tilted its head to one side. This was not a copycat movement, but a deliberate show of defiance. Startled, understandably, I dropped the bottle of iodine, the glass shattering, liquid seeping into the floorboards before I had a chance to properly react. I was dumbfounded. This wasn't an instance of mistaken movement, nor was it easily explained away as a trick of the sudden sunlight shining into the room.

Before I could convince my body to reanimate, the head tilted back to level, and I heard a soft moan escape my lips. My heart felt as if it were attempting to leap out of my chest, to escape the horror I had witnessed. I thought it was over, surely it must be over, but then the shadow bent its knees, crouching near the floor, and raised its head to look directly at me. There was obviously no detail within the darkness, but I could feel it smiling at me. A cold smile that chilled me to my core. I imagined I was living my last moments and watched with increasing disbelief as one arm reached out toward my foot. I watched this with a strange detachment, as if this weren't happening to me, but to someone across the room.

As the hand reached my foot and I felt it begin to tug at my boot, a cloud swallowed up the sun, dimming the room instantly, the shadow losing its grip on me, returning to its mimicry of my actual movements. I breathed then, slowly and deeply, feeling the oxygen rush to my head, making me dizzy. This was the beginning of my paranoia. Although I am quite certain now that paranoia sometimes is our inner logic centers sending alarms to us as a warning.

Three days later I found myself seated across the table from my childhood friend in a dingy pub, trying to find a sane way to explain what had happened. The conversation did not turn out as I had hoped, but nothing he said could convince me that I had misinterpreted my experience. He even went so far as to tell me that he knew a gentleman that dealt in opioids, and he could most likely procure something to help me sleep. *You look simply haggard, dear boy* he said, with concern in his eyes.

I desperately wanted to believe that he was making sense. Nothing would have made me happier than to come to the realization that perhaps I was having a mental breakdown. Yet, there was the nagging itch, unscratchable, etched upon the grooves of my brain that riddled me with doubt. Perhaps it was my shadow trying to convince me of my unwanted clarity regarding its sentience. Whatever the case, I left our conversation feeling decidedly worse about my problem.

All doubt was removed three weeks later. Once again, I had returned to my studies, researching lesser demons, the ones not within the common knowledge of casual interest. The libraries were extremely limited when it came to this type of study, so I had approached a priest within the local archdiocese and requested to review any papers they may have access to within their archives. At first, I had been met with resistance, Father Mulhaney eyeing me suspiciously with a glimmer of real fear hiding behind his expressed trepidation. I had been forced to reveal my involvement in several exorcisms in order for him to budge even the slightest bit. I also assured him that my need for information was purely academic, and that I was planning on publishing my research at a future date and would provide him with a copy to add to his library.

He had eventually relented, allowing me access to the archives, even going so far as to permit me to remove what I found to study in more detail at my home. Of course, he had threatened me with eternal damnation if I were to inadvertently destroy any of the papers during their time away from the church.

What I wouldn't give to have begun with the research at the bottom of the stack. It may have saved me so much trouble, but then again, it may have changed nothing. The cosmic dissonance that had thus far passively swirled about me was about to become much more influential.

I had snatched up a single page paper detailing the dealings of a demon known as Amdusias, a devil responsible for the discordant music used to worship Lucifer in Hell. My skin crawled reading the descriptions of the entity, and when I could no longer maintain my calm, I set my pen down upon the parchment and pressed my thumb and forefinger into the corners of my eyes. That is when I heard the slight scratching sound. At first I imagined it to be another mouse that had found its way inside, but when I opened my eyes, I saw the shadow of my hand reaching for the shadow of my fountain pen, and before I could properly react it had lifted the pen and jammed it into the back of my hand. My mouth went wide in a scream of pain. My vision blurred as tears streamed down my face. I pushed quickly back from the desk, knocking my chair to the floor in the process. My shadow remained in its spot, wielding the shadow pen, waiting for my next move. Somehow, a sense of anticipation sat heavy upon the dark form.

Dashing forward, I snagged the lantern, dousing its light as quickly as I could. And in the last moments before darkness overtook the room, I saw my shadow lunge at my throat with its pen. I closed my eyes and gasped, waiting for the sensation of the sharp implement piercing my throat to end my life. But nothing of the sort occurred. Sweat beaded down my neck as my eyes slowly adjusted to the dimness, the only light filtering in through the windows from the crescent moon. The shadow of my shadow remained attendant to my every move, but I had begun to mistrust this devious creature.

The summer heat baked the earth and its inhabitants, and the fear of allowing my shadow to see the light of day was worsening. I carried a heavy umbrella everywhere I went to ensure that not even an outline of my own shadow could be seen upon the ground.

Colleagues commented on how I could be so pale in the midst of such a heat riddled summer, but I assuaged their concerns by informing them that my research had kept me indoors more than out, and that must be the reasoning for my paleness. Most seemed to accept that explanation, but a few expressed their concerns and made plans to come around my townhome and make sure I got the sunlight I needed.

My good friend Laurence tried to snatch my umbrella from my hand, stating *Why don't you put that damn fool umbrella away and warm yourself up properly.* But he ended his quest when I screamed at him and looked about my person for any sign of extraneous movement. I have not seen Laurence since; I do not believe we are friendly any longer.

For the sake of thoroughness in my tale, I thought I saw my shadow attempt something, but my recovery was too quick for it to follow through and harm me. Which begged the question of whether my shadow was capable of hurting only me or also others, if it had opportunity. This was a line of inquiry I hoped to never have to test. Unfortunately, I found out the answer to my query not long after my altercation with Laurence. Also, I have forgotten to mention that I bandaged my hand after being stabbed and when people asked what had happened, I lacked the courage to speak truthfully, and made up a story about clumsiness and too much drink.

═══════

It wasn't three days later when I became careless enough to incite another incident. This time I feared I would be ended by the sinister entity I had once imagined to be merely a mimic of my own movements. The paranoia had reached the point where I would dodge through doorways, seeking out dark corners in which to hide. I had become nearly vampiric in my activities, which only heightened the concern of those who still considered me a friend or at least an acquaintance.

The sun was making its way steadily below the horizon and I figured that it was a safe time to exit my house. I was lacking in groceries and, with my research reaching the point where I would soon be able to send a draft to a trusted colleague, I convinced myself that a brandy would serve nicely in celebration of my accomplishments. I arrived at the local pub, shoved myself deep into the darkest corner of the establishment, and ordered my drink. What I had not anticipated was running afoul of an ex-love, and even more devastating, she made her way quickly to my table and sat herself across from me.

My mind worked desperately to find a way to extricate myself from this new wrinkle, but before I could recover from the shock of seeing her, the bartender had returned with my brandy and a platter of grilled fruits and cheeses, which I was informed was on the house.

Meanwhile, my unwanted companion commented on how dark it was in this section and wondered if the bartender would be able to find even the slightest bit of light so she could at least see across the table without the necessity of squinting. The bartender nodded and withdrew from the corner to complete his task.

I contemplated draining my glass and leaving, but I felt a hand laid gently upon mine and was compelled to stay. Every word out of her mouth was laced with concern and derision. It felt as though I were a lost puppy, and she was the benevolent soul who would help me out of my situation.

Word about town she intoned, *is that you move about as though you've seen a ghost. You skulk about, jumping from shadow to shadow, hoping to maintain anonymity.* Involuntarily, I jumped each time she mentioned shadows, but I don't believe she noticed. She laid her hand delicately on mine, but it was too much for me to bear. I slowly removed my hand and tented my fingers in front of me on the edge of the table. Her hand remained on the surface, almost as if she were unsure what to do with it.

I had begun to finally relax and believe that maybe everything would be all right when I saw the man bearing a lit oil lamp approaching our table. Without a word he set it down and departed. Instantly, my shadow leapt up behind me and I could feel its presence. With one swift motion, the shadow of the knife that had been laid out with the charcuterie was snatched up and brought down on the pinky finger of the woman sitting across the table. She shrieked in agony, blood spurting forth from the stump of where her finger had once been.

All eyes turned to me as I attempted to staunch the flow of blood using a handkerchief I kept in my jacket pocket. I attempted to focus all my attention on my guest, but the soft murmurs around the establishment infiltrated my concentration. Words of accusation and cries for the police filled the space immediately. My companion looked faint, the color drained from her face, and I could see the indictment in her eyes. The initial shock wore off and she pulled herself away from me, backing into the center of the room, before collapsing.

I thought for sure this would be my end. I would be arrested and thrown in jail, where I wouldn't be able to control how much or how little light I would have to endure. A cadre of gentlemen approached me, hands outstretched, trying to convince me they meant me no harm. My mouth moved silently, my head shaking back and forth trying to inform them that I had not done anything. But even as the scene played out, I knew there was zero chance of anyone believing my tale. I accepted my fate and allowed the men to bring me to the floor and hold me there until the police arrived and escorted me away. The entire process was terrifying, but my shadow remained passive until five days later, when the lady I had been accused of cutting off her finger finally came around enough to doubt that I had actually done anything. She had no explanation for what had occurred, but her recollection of events did not coincide with the accusations leveled at me.

Much to my relief I was released in the middle of the night, and I snaked my way back home using the darkness of alleys and coverings to keep my shadow at bay. A plan had begun to form, and I set about implementing it the very next day.

As summer silently ended and the infinite colors of Autumn made themselves known I had earned the title of the town recluse. I rarely ventured outdoors, and when I did I made sure my shadow wouldn't be able to make an unwanted appearance. This made it seem as though I was avoiding any possible human contact, which was a fair assessment. I didn't believe that I could live with myself if my shadow were to hurt another person.

Children crossed to the other side of the street when they saw me approaching, men and women lowered their voices conspiratorially, making only snatches of conversation audible to me. I would hear words like *insane* and *dangerous* escape people's lips. It made me angry, but the fear of my shadow outweighed my desire to prove my stable mind.

Since caution had become tantamount to my existence, any slip of a moment where I was not diligent, I would see my shadow reach for me, try to strangle me, to hurt me in some way that would prevent me from keeping it hidden. Often, I would feel the sensation of fingertips upon the back of my neck or notice a breath in my ear. I developed tics where I would swat at the nothingness surrounding me, which I know only enhanced the stories the others would tell.

Desperate, I procured a stack of wooden boards and nailed them over every window that could allow light to enter my home. I learned the layout of my house well enough to traverse it safely in pitch darkness. There wasn't even enough ambient light to allow my eyes to adjust to the infinite black that settled into that space. Citizens, concerned for my well-being, although I am fairly certain they had concern only for themselves or the ones they loved, sent the police around on a regular basis. I would speak to them through my door, not daring to venture out into the street unless absolutely necessary.

The problem with the lifestyle I adopted was I could no longer do my research. My fear had become so attuned to my existence that any flicker of light would cause me to break out in a cold sweat. I have never been a religious man, but I convinced myself that if I studied within the walls of the church there was a spiritual binding that wouldn't allow unnatural occurrences. It seemed to work, because I was able to continue my studies unaffected, but I could feel a malevolent force held at bay, waiting for its opportunity to destroy.

Winter had arrived, and I was reaching the last of the papers in the stack I had originally procured from the church archives. A sense of relief and accomplishment washed over me, releasing months of tension that had been building. Maybe after my book was complete, I could retire to a cave and live in unrelenting darkness the rest of my life.

I grabbed at a piece of paper, but it was stuck in the stack. There was a moment where I almost gave up and reached for another page, but for some reason I felt compelled to succeed in extracting this information from the pile. That is when I discovered the key to what was happening to me.

The page was handwritten and barely legible. Either the hand that had put pen to paper was old, or the person who had written it was terrified and in a hurry to share the information with whomever needed it.

At the top of the page was written: *Invidiak – The Shadow Demon.* My blood ran cold and my breathing shallowed. The presence of my shadow shifted enough to inform me that I was onto something important. As I read, I learned that the invidiak was a shapeshifting demon that hides its presence within shadows. Somehow one of these entities had attached itself to *my* shadow and was slowly terrorizing me. I thought back to the exorcisms I had been present for and wondered if I had not received this curse as a residual side effect of spiritual warfare during one of the sessions.

A deep rage filled my body, and I shook with fury at the violation that had been forced upon me. In my research I had discovered that demonic entities were only able to take possession of a person through invitation. Yet, the demon had not taken possession of me, but rather my shadow. I was unlearned when it came to the semantics of what constituted a person or something related to a person, but not attuned to their soul. The more I read the more I felt the demon attempt to dissuade me from the knowledge, for that is truly the only way to defeat a creature such as this. *Know thine enemy.* I devoured the page again and again, looking for hidden messages, subtext that could assist me in ridding myself of this malicious entity. Nothing stood out, but I had more firepower than I did before. I simply needed to fine tune my newfound knowledge into a weapon.

I reached out to the only person I knew that might be able to acquit me of this devilry.

And now I sit in my house, darkness surrounding me like a blanket, waiting for my visitor. Waiting with multiple lanterns filled and ready to expose the Invidiak.

After I explained to Father Mulhaney the affliction I suffered, he informed me he needed to pray and seek counsel and would return to me in five days to give me an answer. He seemed to believe every word I said. I hope he believed every word I said. I need him to believe every word I said.

The build up of tension I have felt over the last hours is surely the demon's attempt at frightening me off of this line of action. If not for the utter darkness, I know this entity would rip me limb from limb. Maybe its arrogance led it to become lax in its dealings with me. Perhaps the terror it filled me with is how it feeds. Either way, I plan on ending this tonight. All I need is Father Mulhaney to arrive and help me finish my story. One way or another.

There is a knock at the door. I jump, anxiety setting my nerves on edge. Then nothing. Perhaps I am hearing things. But then, the knocking again, more urgent than before. The time has come. The moment of passing from reality into another. I lift myself from my chair and take a deep breath. My feet move to the door, the intimate knowledge of any obstacles second nature. I grab the handle of the door and close my eyes.

God, I hope this works.

THE BLACK STONE JOURNAL

The following pages are excerpts from a journal that was found on the Hillerby Ranch ten miles outside of Mossy Rock, Washington. The entries have been typed for the sake of clarity, and any sections that were difficult to read have been notated with an asterisk at the beginning and end of stated section.

Not much is known about Michael Hillerby aside from the entries into his journal that mention he was a former agent for a few actors in Hollywood and had decided to cut ties with that old life and start fresh raising animals and tending a garden.

For the sake of brevity, only the most relevant entries have been included in this manuscript. Anything omitted was deemed unnecessary exposition detailing the day-to-day struggles with running a small farm. There are a few exceptions that are either used to establish context or are included in a relevant entry.

What follows is a disturbing account of a man seemingly descending into madness. Unfortunately, there is no way to verify anything in this journal as Michael Hillerby has not been located. After an extensive search was conducted through the woods surrounding Hillerby Ranch, the only possible evidence that was found was an object that matched the description around which this entire journal is centered.

The search lasted nearly a month before it was called off and Michael Hillerby was declared deceased.

Readers are encouraged to use their own discretion if they choose to continue past this point.

SEPTEMBER 19, 2020

I finally got my shipment of animals. Well, shipment seems like an odd word to use when referring to living creatures, but I honestly don't know how else to put it. Delivery? Doesn't matter.

Two goats, one milk cow, one bull, a pair of sheep, a few ducks, and a shit-ton of chickens.

They arrived all together on a large trailer pulled by an absolutely beefy looking truck. The driver was not a well-spoken man or at least didn't seem to be, because he did a lot of nodding and shaking his head. He gave me a couple tips on animal husbandry, and spat his tobacco juice onto the ground to emphasize his points.

It took nearly two hours to get the animals off the trailer and into their respective housing situations. The damned chicken coop still wasn't quite secure enough and thank God only a few escaped before farmer Phil (that's what he said to call him) left. He was able to help button up the escape hatches so I wouldn't have to worry about it anymore.

After an admonition to be wary of predators in the woods, he went on his merry way and I checked in on all the creatures, great and small. I haven't decided on names yet and I doubt I'll try to name all the chickens, but I'm almost settled on The Great Hornholio for the bull, because he has a massive set of horns. Very apropos.

I was surprised when the sun began to slide behind the trees and decided to walk the perimeter of the forest to make sure my animals would be able to roam the land without having to worry about them disappearing into the woods, never to return.

The fencing all looked solid, and the two gates that led off into different sections of the forest were shut and locked. Everything was normal, except for the goats. I found them standing near the electrified fence bordering a dense part of the woods and staring in. It took a few gentle whacks to their rumps to shock them out of their stupor and I was able to put them in their pen before retiring for the night.

James texted me and said he would be out in mid-October to stay for a few days. I honestly don't know if this is a good idea or not, but it will be nice to see an actual friend from my old life.

The wind started blowing while I was writing this. I hope nothing falls down overnight.

That would suck.

SEPTEMBER 26, 2020

I've made it nearly a week and haven't lost a single animal. Maybe this endeavor will turn out to not be the worst mistake of my life. The chickens are too smart. Should've asked for a dumber breed. They keep escaping, but none of them have tried the great escape into the woods.

Over the week I have caught different animals peering into the forest, sometimes for hours at a time. I think I mentioned how weird that was a couple days ago. Today, The Great Hornholio stood for nearly three hours in one spot and when I went up to him saliva was dripping out of his mouth, and he was making a panting sound. I have given up trying to lure them out of their trances, because they always eventually do it on their own. Everybody likes to sleep snugly in their enclosures.

The wild grass and bushes are nearly cleared in the southwest corner of the property. Thank God for non-picky eaters. Maybe I won't end up having to buy a lawnmower after all. It'll definitely take them at least a few months to gobble it all up, but winter is around the corner, so nothing else will grow for a while.

I know most of these entries have been focused solely on the animals and how they're acclimating to their new lives, but that's partially because I have been dreading putting down on paper the other piece of all this.

Ugh.

Here goes.

I have been having ~~dreams~~ nightmares. Like, really bad nightmares. Most of them have to do with stepping out of my house in the morning to find all my animals slaughtered. Thousands of dollars dead and gone before I even had a chance to earn money at the local farmer's market. That sounds so callous and flippant. I get it. Like I said when I started this journal, I have enough reserves to last me a long time, but at some point I will need to find a way to make some money or this lifestyle won't be sustainable. So, why not stay ahead of that deadly curve and plan accordingly?

The worst part of the nightmares is the humming sound. It is constant, unbroken, and makes it feel like my teeth are vibrating. I'm fairly certain I clench my teeth every time I have one of these nightmares, because when I wake up my jaw aches and my gums are super sensitive.

Last night's dream, and the reason I have decided to stop putting off journaling about it, I left the house in bare feet, but there were no dead animals outside my front door. I was confused, because apparently *dream me* remembers the other nightmares and fully expected to come across piles of carcasses. Instead of returning to the comfort of the dream bed, *dream me* decided to do a little exploring. The hum persisted. No matter where *dream me* went on the property.

Dream me walked across the field toward the forest and in the dim light of the quarter moon saw what appeared to be fallen branches and leaves stuck to the fence. As *dream me* got closer and closer it became apparent that it was in fact the viscera of the animals.

I tried to get through to *dream me* in order to get him to back off and go back to the house and go back to sleep, but he was having none of it. Helplessly, I watched him approach the fence and saw that it looked like something had tried to pull the poor creatures through the wires. I don't want to get too graphic, but it was like someone had tried to shove a hotdog through a straw, but with a lot more fur and feathers.

Dream me looked around and saw one of the goats was still alive. But it reared up on its hind legs like it was going to headbutt *dream me* and that's when I woke up, screaming. Maybe I should go see a doctor. I wonder if they have a sleeping pill that will keep the nightmares away.

SEPTEMBER 27, 2020

Had yet another nightmare last night.

Woke up to find my feet were filthy and so were my sheets.

Don't feel much like journaling today.

Shit.

SEPTEMBER 30, 2020

It finally happened! One of the goats made it into the woods. I don't know how he did it, because I have triple-checked the fence and gates and there is no way, unless he figured out how to jump six feet in the air to clear the electric wire. Stupid *unreadable* goat!

After checking to make sure none of the other animals had Steve McQueened their way into the woods, I set out to find the wayward little shit.

I discovered quite a few trails, most of them overgrown with small plant life, but there was one trail that led to a small pond in a little clearing. There was nothing spectacular about the pond, except for the shiny black rock that almost seemed to serve as a marker for the place. It was the deepest shade of black I have ever seen. Like, it felt as though I could reach out and into the stone. Like I could disappear inside it. I had trouble reconciling the lack of light creating a cave or hole-like illusion and the solidity of the rock when I reached out and touched it. My fingertips thrummed with some heavy energy that emanated from deep within the stone and I pulled back quickly.

As soon as I took a few steps back from the rock I could feel that thrumming dissipating. And that's when I noticed the goat. Apparently I had been so focused on this object that I hadn't even seen my goat standing with his face inches from the thing, mesmerized. It startled me. I won't lie. I may have jumped and made some inarticulate noises. I may have peed a little. Who knows.

Anyhow, I was able to coax the goat to return to the farm with me using a leash and a bundle of oats. Once he was nestled into his enclosure, I went into the house, done for the day.

I debated with myself on whether to include this, because it seems silly. The day probably simply slipped away from me. But, if I'm going for posterity here I should probably mention it. When I entered the woods, it was just after lunch. I remember, because I told myself that I would eat the last steak in my fridge to give myself the protein boost I would inevitably need to conduct a thorough search and rescue. ~~This is stupid.~~ By the time I got back into the house it was nearly 10pm.

Now, I know it didn't take me nearly 10 hours to find my stupid goat. I know it. But I don't know where the rest of the day went. How did I not notice that it was dark when I led my stupid goat back to his pen? Why wasn't I particularly hungry even though the last morsel of food I ate was around noon? I'm writing this down at 11:58pm.

You know that creepy crawly sensation you get when something feels like it's sitting half an inch to the left of reality? Everything is normal, but… not quite? That's what this feels like. The goat is safe. I am safe. Every other animal is safe. Nothing actually happened.

But it feels like everything unseen happened. And it's sending shivers up my spine as I write about it.

OCTOBER 4, 2020

Today was fairly normal. But I can't stop thinking about that black rock by the pond in the forest. I've been back out there a few times, I don't know why. Maybe I was trying to recreate the time warp I experienced last week. But it hasn't happened. At least not in any significant way.

The stone has a magnetism to it. I am drawn to it. I don't know how to properly explain the feeling, but try to imagine a gravity well. If I could visualize the pull of the rock I think it would look like a series of vibrating ripples moving slowly toward it. Or, maybe it's like something from a movie where somebody is gradually getting sucked through a vortex. It's not as intense as that, but it's how it FEELS to me.

I have begun eating lunch by the pond, leaned up against the stone. ~~I wish it would whisper its secrets to me.~~ It is very relaxing.

On another note I can't find one of my chickens. Maybe I should have named them so I could figure out which one is missing, but whatever. I have a whole gaggle of them left. I guess it's just another excuse to wander the forest again. But what happens if I find the dead body of that chicken? What do I do with that information? I wonder what happened to the family that lived here before. I only know it was a family because that's what I was told when I bought the place. The real estate agent was very cagey about them, saying they preferred to remain out of the process as much as possible, for privacy. I tried to pry, but the agent held firm because of the former owner's wishes.

Maybe tomorrow I will go into town and see if I can find anything out. I suspect the stone has something to do with the previous owners wanting to sell the property. Just an idea that's been niggling at me ~~for a while~~ lately.

James will be here a week from today. I hope to show him the black rock. I think he would get a kick out of it. Maybe we will picnic by the pond every day he is here, which is supposed to be two whole weeks. I'm still a bit nervous about letting someone from my past life enter into my new one. But I'm sure it'll be fine.

Everything's gonna be fine.

~~I hope~~

OCTOBER 5, 2020

I did it. I went into town. Who knew they still used microfiche? I found an article about how the two children that lived on my property had gone missing and an extensive search was done but had never turned anything up. There was one section that caught my eye specifically: When questioned about the last time he saw his children, Manny replied, "I know what did it. I know exactly what made my children disappear. It was the midnight rock. The midnight rock did it."

I mean, he's got to mean the black stone, right? Midnight Rock, Black stone? Seems like they are one and the same.

After they discontinued the search the children's mother had gone away to live with her sister, unable to shake the unimaginable grief she was feeling. The father had been committed to a Sanitarium in his home state of Idaho. He kept raving about his midnight rock and how if he could just get it to open up he could find his children and save them. Everyone thought he was crazy and when I mentioned his name to the librarian she shook her head and said that the whole thing was such a tragedy.

On a completely different note it would have been nice to know a couple children went missing from the place I now call my home. Seriously? I thought real estate agents had to disclose information like that, but when I called my agent she told me that because they had simply disappeared there was no "Death Disclosure" needed. I could practically see the air quotes when she said it. Then she told me that technically Washington state doesn't have a "Death Disclosure" clause, so she wouldn't have had to say anything even if the bodies had been found.

Why do people have to be so shady? It doesn't make sense.

I came back to the ranch and visited the Black Stone, which is what I have decided to name it. Or…nah. My head was swimming and I needed a break from the craziness that had been happening since I came across the Black Stone. I decided to take a dip in the pond, au natural of course. Who was going to see me? The pull of the water was irresistible. And it definitely felt healing on my tired body and mind. ~~There is a little algae in the pond, but not enough to cause any problems.~~ The algae isn't too bothersome. Maybe I'll try and take some home with me. I know people like to use algae in cooking. Or maybe the animals will like it.

Not today. I was too tired by the time I got out of the pond to do much else but shower, shave and eat a microwave dinner.

The nightmares are back. But the humming has subsided a bit. It's almost soothing now.

OCTOBER 9, 2020

The animals are disappearing at a rapid rate. What the hell is going on? I don't understand this. I still have a couple chickens, but The Great Horn-holio has somehow managed to escape the field. And the milk cow isn't producing milk. She backs away from me when I come close. Stupid cow. Why did I do this? What is the point? I feel so ~~dumb~~ ~~inadequate~~ tired. There is something to be said about trying new things, and persevering, and all that shit. But I just don't know about... THIS... anymore. The sheep are fine and I'm pretty certain the ducks are all gone. I did find one swimming in the pond this morning. I tried to shoo it away. It was disrupting the tranquility. How dare it swim in such a sacred spot. What sacrilege. Speaking of sacrilege, I think I almost heard the Black Stone whisper to me today. I placed my ear against it's midnight skin and felt the thrum through the entirety of my head. But I digress. I really wish

So, I just had a visitor at the door. I'm starting a new line, because I want to distinguish this part of my entry from the previous one. This visitor, at first I thought it was one of my goats, but I don't have black goats. One is all white and the other has splotches of brown on white hair. This one was almost the same level of dark as the Black Stone. And it stood on its hind legs. I don't mean it reared up on them, I mean when I opened the door the damn thing was standing, like a human, waiting for me. I wouldn't have been surprised if it had spoken to me. I mean, kind of it did. I'm not saying I heard an audible voice speak to me, but... I don't know, more of a feeling than anything else. I swear it was trying to tell me that it would protect me. From what or who? Dunno. Just a feeling.

OCTOBER 11, 2020

If I'm being honest I kind of regret letting James stay here for a couple weeks. I mean, he is one of my dearest friends, ~~and one of the only actors in Hollywood who was genuinely a good person~~ That's not fair. There are a lot of nice people in Hollywood. But he had an integrity that couldn't be corrupted. Which is probably why I'm regretting this whole visit. Oh well, it's too late. He arrived this morning and got settled into the guest bedroom.

I showed him around the ranch and when we got to the gate I usually walk through to visit the Black Stone I hurried him on by. What right does HE have to gaze upon such an incredible artifact? He'll probably go blab it around California and then I would be inundated with lookie-loos who just wanted to get a singular glimpse.

Therefore, I have resolved to not tell him about it at all. Once he is gone I will go visit the Black Stone and ~~apologize for my absence~~ make sure everything is a-ok. I have two chickens left, my goats are still sticking it out, and the sheep simply act like nothing is happening… ever. The milk cow has flown the coop, so to speak. Good riddance. I didn't need an extra mouth to feed with nothing in return.

James enjoyed touring the property and even had a few good suggestions for things I could do with the land: Grow corn and pumpkins and have the locals visit during October for hayrides and maze exploring and pumpkin picking. Obviously this would be a next year kind of deal, since October is almost already half over.

Another idea he had was learning to can and jar things so I could sell them at the local farmer's market. That was an idea with legs. It would take quite a bit of work, but I could make some good money from pickled beets, jams, creamed corn, whatever my heart desires.

Now that I'm thinking about it, I don't want people coming to my property and "accidentally" running across the Black Stone. That's for me and me alone. It's special. ~~It told me so. It lives~~ It's on my property and it is a privilege to keep it as my little secret.

Maybe I can still sneak out to the woods while James is asleep and visit the Black Stone. That will calm my jangling nerves. That will put everything into perspective.

I can hear James snoring down the hall. This is going to be a long two weeks.

OCTOBER 13, 2020

Today's entry is simply going to be a conversation I had with James. I am so frustrated that he is staying another week and a half. I shouldn't have agreed to this. But, I need to write this conversation down while it is still fresh in my mind.

James: A lot of people miss you back home.
Me: I get that, but I had to do this for myself.
James: Yep. And I see why after being here only a couple days. There is a level of peace that could never be acquired in L.A. I haven't slept this well in years. Maybe I'll find some property near here and move—
Me: No.
James: Damn. I didn't even finish the sentence. Why not?
Me: No properties available, that's all.
James: Sounded more personal.
Me: No.
James: Okay. I was only half-serious anyhow. I think I would go a little crazy this far from civilization.
Me: I'm not crazy.
James: I never said you were crazy. I was speaking personally.
Me: Of course. My apologies. I'm just a little tired. I told you about my animals. That's been a little stressful is all.
James: Yeah, that would be stressful.
Me: Nothing like the stresses in Cali, eh?
James: Not even close, my friend.

We had a long moment of silence before he continued.

James: You ever hike through the forest?
Me: Yeah, there's nothing much. A lot of trees. I've hardly even seen any

wildlife. Most of the paths are overgrown.
James: It's got a nice little pond though, yeah?

This took me by surprise. And then I got angry. Irrationally angry, because obviously he was a guest at my house and there was no good reason to keep him from wandering the woods. Except now he knew about the Black Stone.

Me: Sure. That too.
James: So you've seen the rock that looks almost too dark to be real.
Me: I have.
James: I've never seen a color that deep before. I didn't think anything on Earth could achieve that level of darkness.
Me: It's crazy, huh?
James: Totally.
Me: I'm hungry.
James: Me too. Let's eat.

So, now he knows about the Black Stone. What am I going to do? I can't just ~~keep him~~ have him move in or something. And he's rich, so bribery won't do it.

I guess that leaves blackmail.

OCTOBER 15, 2020

Oh shit. Oh God. What… what… why?

The broken(?) amulet. The flying crate! I need to calm down. Deep breaths. Writing this down helps. Okay. Ummmmmmmmmmmmmmmmmmmm… I don't really know how to put this.

The goat is not a goat. Yeah. The goat is not a goat. The one that walks on its hindlegs? Not a goat. It is some interdimensional demon. I was walking toward the pond with James. Dusk was approaching. We didn't make it until the sun had set. I felt the call of the Black Stone. I had to resist. I couldn't let James know the power it held. I couldn't let on that there was something more to it than anyone could understand.

So, we sit, toes dangling in the water, talking about the old life. Reminiscing. And the goat… demon… thing appears at the edge of the clearing. James doesn't see him at first. I try to shoo it away. I try to make it understand it should not be seen by this other person. Not walking on two legs.

But James notices. He notices and turns directly toward it. He was immediately terrified. Backed right up into me and I moved out of the way, words stuck in my throat. I couldn't tell him it was okay. I couldn't convince him the goat… demon… thing wasn't harmful.

Oh god. Oh godddd.

It opened up its mouth to reveal *several rows of razor* sharp teeth. I guess it would be called *a maw* at that point. But the thing opened its mouth wider and taller than it should have been capable of doing. And it lunged at James. James didn't have *any seconds* to jump out of the way and it latched onto his throat. I've heard stories of the chupacabra, and I felt like this was some sort of reverse thing. It sucked him dry. Only bones and bits of sinew remained when it was done.

And then it strode back into the forest like nothing happened. What the hell? What the hell? What the HELL??!!

I feel like I'm going crazy. That I'm seeing hallucinations around every corner. And now The Black Stone is covered in blood. In my friend's blood. I have to remedy that tomorrow. The Black Stone should do nothing but shine… or suck away the light. Whichever it does.

I doubt I'm going to sleep tonight. I don't know if I'll ever sleep again. I think I need to move.

Why didn't the goat… demon… thing come after me?

OCTOBER 16, 2020

The blood was gone. All gone. None on The Black Stone, none in the dirt around the area. Only the bones. The bones of my friend. I chucked them into the pond. I thought it seemed fitting. I mean, I can't tell the police what happened. Who's gonna believe that an interdimensional demon ate my friend? So, the pond I thought would be the move. I don't know what else to do.

While I was clearing the area I felt the pull of the Black Stone. It sank its hooks into me and lulled me into a trance. It allowed me to see inside it. Into the deep abyss with endless corridors of nothingness for all eternity. I wallowed in the shallow end of the universe brought full circle. Time did not exist. If anything it ran parallel to itself in a triple helix, time and space and infinity. I could feel the granules of the atoms slipping through my fingers like loose sand on the beach. Gaping into the maw of eternity, I felt as though I didn't even exist. I was the merest speck of dust on the glass plane of existence. One swipe and I wouldn't have ever been. One false move and my history would be erased. The enormity of it stole away my breath leaving me gasping, praying for it all to end.

And then it released me. The demon stood beside me, its mouth opened wide, the rows of teeth shining in the daylight. It seemed to want me to become lost inside it, but I closed my eyes and breathed deeply until the feeling subsided. I had witnessed too much, and anything more surely would drive me into the arms of madness.

So, I fled from the pond. I returned to my house. My mind was still affected by my experience. Even when I squeezed my eyes shut, I saw it.

I shuttered the windows and locked the doors. I flipped the breaker boxes to rid the house of its insidious hum. I sat in the middle of the floor of my living room and heard the faint scratching of something at my door. I closed my eyes in an attempt to drown out everything but the void.

And I screamed.

OCTOBER 20, 2020

The children have been on my mind a lot lately. ~~I need to save them.~~ I feel as though I can find them. I feel as though they are still alive. There is proof to be found, but I must revisit the Black Stone. That object that once filled me with awe and jealousy had begun to reveal its wickedness, its horrors. What once was pleasure now was sinister.

Yet the demon will not allow me to avoid the pond. He is at my doorstep every morning, mouth agape, razor teeth glistening with saliva. I fear that if I do not obey its commands, it will swallow me whole and leave nothing but my bones to bear witness to my existence. I have become *unnaturally* terrified. *Unnaturally* paranoid.

But I know I need to investigate. Deeper. I know I need to unlock the secrets that the Black Stone holds so dearly. There is a void *unreadable* the end of all humanity. I sense it, like a primal instinct.

Today I followed the demon to the pond and stood beside the Black Stone for hours, unmoving. In the beginning I couldn't tell how long I had been entranced by the Black Stone, but now I felt every agonizing moment. It was a painful experience. But I believe I caught a glimpse of something I had never seen before. I could be wrong. It could have been a trick of the light. It's entirely possible that I willed myself to see something there. But I will test my theory tomorrow. Tomorrow feels important. Tomorrow feels inevitable. Tomorrow feels like the beginning of the end. I will have my answers, for better or worse. Maybe the demon will *relieve itself of* my presence, move on to torture another.

There is nothing left to do but hope and pray.

OCTOBER 21, 2020

THE BLACK STONE DID IT! THE

BLACK STONE DID IT! THE BLACK STONE DID

IT! THE BLACK STONE DID IT!

(The rest of this entry has been cut short, but the repeated phrase filled an entire notebook)

OCTOBER 31, 2020

I have purchased my supplies. There is a sinking sensation in my stomach that tells me no matter how prepared I am I still will not be prepared enough. But I must try. The children need me. I can find them and save them.

Set before me on the floor are:

- Two ropes
- A backpack
- Flares
- Food
- Water Bottles
- Knives
- A pistol and ammunition
- Two flashlights

Looking at it makes it seem like it's not enough. But it will have to do. This must be done tonight, or I will lose my nerve. I'm afraid I may be losing it while I write this. But I have to make my statement before I enter the Black Stone.

My name is Michael Hillerby. I am of sound body and mind. At midnight tonight I will tie a rope to a tree near the pond and enter the Black Stone. I will not return until I have found the children who lived on this property before me. If I do not return, my land is to be sold and the proceeds are to go to the hospital where the children's father resides.

I must finish my preparations. If I fail to return, let these journals serve as my story. It's funny how when I first ran across the Black Stone I felt the need to keep it hidden and secret. But now I feel that I must warn as many as I can about its insidious nature. Please stay away from the Black Stone. It's not worth it.

This was the last entry in Michael Hillerby's journals. The bones of his friend were found in the pond, but Michael was never found, nor was the rope he wrote he would tie around a tree before 'entering the black stone'.

THE WOOD WILL SWALLOW
YOU WHOLE

Trevor Morris found a small, obscure parking spot just past a ditch on the main road and tucked his old Ford in as best he could. He was aware that the land he was approaching was not public, and even if it had been, what he was about to do would have been 'frowned upon'. It had even crossed his mind that it might be punishable with a fine or time in prison. But, typical of Trevor, he kept his intentions and indiscretions to himself.

There was one steadfast rule he lived by when it came to his excursions into the forest: only carry what would fit inside the knapsack he was holding. He had overloaded on one occasion and that had almost ended in disaster. It was not an experience he planned on duplicating.

Checking both directions down the potholed road, he didn't see or hear any other vehicles. It had taken him the better part of two hours to find this spot, and the specific trees he was looking for. In that moment he was relieved and satisfied.

Trevor crossed the road, basking in the quiet of early afternoon. There was the occasional bird call and scurrying of some small animal in the underbrush, but other than that it was completely silent. There wasn't even a breeze to rustle the leaves.

Another rule, by which he tried to abide, was choosing a spot where he could quickly return to his truck should things go sideways. Fortunately for him there was a direct path leading to one of the trees he was looking for: the White Oak. He used this tree, because the roots were incredibly thick and sturdy, which served his purposes well.

At the trailhead he noticed a sign tacked to a small tree. The sign read:

NO TRESPASSERS! YOU HAVE BEEN WARNED!

Trevor chuckled to himself and rolled his eyes. He was certain no one was going to come to this specific part of the forest checking for interlopers. If someone did make it that far, hopefully the sign would scare them off.

He continued down the trail and within a hundred yards he had reached one of the most magnificent White Oaks he had ever seen. Looking up he could hardly see the top branches. If he had to guess, it was close to a hundred feet. This was an old tree. It had lived long enough to acquire a history.

Setting his knapsack on the ground, he placed both hands on the trunk of the tree. He knew in the long run he wasn't hurting the trees; they had so many roots that chopping a few to make his furniture didn't make a difference. And he always made sure to move from one White Oak to another to prevent any from rotting. He wouldn't want to harm this resource.

Trevor took a deep breath and stated, barely above a whisper, "I'm not here to harm you. I simply wish to utilize your natural strength and beauty."

The first few times he had spoken to one of the trees he was planning on hewing, he felt quite silly. But, it had now become an important part of his ritual. Respect the tree and the tree respected you; at least, that's how he justified what he was doing.

Trevor next knelt down and placed his hands on the mossy ground surrounding the base of the White Oak, and said, "Thank you for your gifts."

He opened his knapsack and took out a small saw, a hammer and chisel, a trowel, and a crowbar. Placing them in a line in next to him, he took a deep breath and closed his eyes. He stayed that way for a long while, centering himself in nature.

Finally, he opened his eyes, exhaled, grabbed the trowel, and began to dig around the trunk. The ground was soft and loose, making the work easy. Within mere moments he had exposed a tangle of roots. He smiled. Tiny stragglers meant a large, thick root was nearby.

Setting the trowel aside, he dug in with his hands and pulled up through the root feelers. Suddenly, he was overwhelmed by the smell of fresh earth and it carried him…

The morning sun peeked through the window of Trevor's one bedroom apartment. A stray beam of light did its best to pierce his eyelids as he slept, and after a minute or two it succeeded, eliciting a grunt.

He screened his face with his hand to block the brightness to let his blurred vision clear up before trying to get out of bed. His girlfriend was still asleep and he carefully rose, hoping not to wake her.

Taking a deep breath, he inhaled her perfume and sighed contentedly. She must have been wearing it the night before, but he couldn't properly remember. Too much alcohol.

He looked at her and a moment of indecision passed. He had to pee, but he also wanted to go back to sleep for a few hours. His stomach grumbled, but his bed looked entirely too cozy to ignore. There was a scratch at the back of his throat, but the bed was calling to him.

He gave up and crawled into the bed and and snuggled up to his girlfriend. When he wrapped his arms tightly around her, she sighed in her sleep. He put his chin on her shoulder, nuzzling into the crook of her neck and inhaled deeply, taking in the wonderful scent of his girlfriend's perfume.

He had just settled into a comfortable position when shedecided to shift and whacked him right on the ear. It startled him and…

Trevor sharply inhaled and he was momentarily confused. He blinked his eyes and remembered. He was kneeling in front of a White Oak, the sounds of the forest comforting him, and his fingers were in the dirt. He took a deep breath, relieved.

Yet, his fingers weren't *resting* in the dirt. They were tangled in the root tendrils and it took Trevor considerable amount of effort to free them.

He was surprised he had been daydreaming. Never before had he drifted off while digging for his treasure. It didn't make sense. His girlfriend had broken up with him nearly a year prior, refusing to even speak to him after she moved out. Why was he reminiscing about her *now*?

Shaking his head to clear it, Trevor bent forward to his task once again, removing some of the smaller roots to begin to expose the one that was barely beyond reach.

After a minute, he was sweating from the exertion of digging and yanking, and sat back on his heels, wiping sweat with the back of his gloved hand.

It took him too long to realize that the sounds of the forest had disappeared. That was the best way he could describe it. It was as if every creature and leaf and blade of grass had agreed they no longer wanted to exist in this spot, and took their whispers, rustles, hoots and whistles elsewhere.

The hair rose on the back of his neck. Trevor was anxious, and chills climbed up his spine. It felt as though he were being watched; that someone else was in the woods. An ominous presence somewhere outside his line of sight.

Very casually – at least in Trevor's mind – he stretched, and as he did, glanced quickly around looking for any sign of movement. But there was nothing. No one stepped out from behind a tree. No creature made a sound or moved. Nothing was out there with him. He was asl alone now as when he had arrived.

Comforted by this knowledge, even if his nerves were still jangling a bit, he returned to his work. He saw that the smallest roots were now out of the way, exposing one of the bigger roots. Using his crowbar, he hooked it around the root whose circumference was about that of a rolled up yoga mat. He then attempted to lever the root into a more accessible position.

It took some grunting and sweat, but he succeeded in maneuvering it where he wanted. Trevor smiled. A beautiful root lay bare in front of him.

He grabbed the handsaw and gently placed the teeth of the blade on the top of the root. Patting the root in a way he hoped was caring and honoring, he applied a slight amount of pressure to the handle and pushed it away from his body.

The sound of the saw breaching the outer layer of the root was like music to Trevor's ears. He closed his eyes, listening and feeling it slowly give way under the blade. Inhaling the earthy air around him, he continued to cut, allowing the teeth to do most of the work. He was saving his energy for the next step.

Trevor took another deep breath, sensing a change in the aroma of the forest. He smelled a scent that didn't belong. At first, he couldn't place it. It didn't belong here; almost discordant. It carried him…

It was the salty air of the ocean that accosted Trevor's nostrils, making him cough. His toes were firmly buried in the sand as he watched the tide roll in and out, dancing to its own internal rhythm. He was lost in a reverie.

This trip had been an escape from his normal life, where he lived as an office worker from 9 to 5, five days a week, and was a boyfriend the rest of the time. At some point he realized that he was slowly dying. Truly living hadn't been a viable option for a long time. Instead it was: wake up, make enough money to survive, take care of others, rinse and repeat.

When he had informed his girlfriend that he was planning on taking a month off to go to the beach, she was very excited. Excited, until he told her he was going alone. That was probably the first rift in their relationship. She had always been sour and resentful when he returned home from one of his trips. When less and less met her expectations, she became increasingly suspicious. Trevor imagined she believed he was cheating on her with another woman; the beach trip simply a cover. No matter how many times he attempted to quell her fears, she would eventually burst into tears or shut him down with a passive-aggressive jab. That succeeded in pissing him off to the point that he went for a walk to cool off, and always slammed the door as he left.

The plus side was he got a lot of exercise, but the negatives definitely outweighed the positives. They lasted another two months before she called it quits. Trevor wondered if his announcement played a big part in her decision. Probably. By then he was mostly angry and she was mostly disappointed. It was a relief when he came home and she wasn't there.

Trevor was quitting his job to focus on woodworking. The beach trip was important, even necessary.

At the beginning of Trevor's spiritual journey he had met a man who made the most stunning sculptures out of wood, flowing objects that couldn't possibly have been made by human hands. The works were flawless, and Trevor believed that if he could even produce something half as amazing, he would always be fine, by himself.

During that time he spent most of his days watching the woodworker closely; figuring out the tricks he employed to make his art so aesthetically pleasing. He tried to decipher the small movements that joined the pieces together with so little effort. It was the first time Trevor had learned anything that completely consumed his attention. He wasn't simply interested in the work, he was fascinated and overtaken by it.

When he wasn't with the woodworker, he would sit on the beach and allow the waves to lull him into a contemplative state of mind. Looking back Trevor was convinced that trip saved his life, gave him purpose, and set his bones on fire with a desire to create.

At that moment, a rogue wave soaked Trevor to his waist. Shocked by the icy water, he snapped awake.

Shuddering as a chill passed through his entire body, he glanced around to reorient himself. As if he was listening for further instructions, his face was inches from the White Oak he had been working on.

He rested his head on the bark for a moment he attempted, but when he attempted to sit straight up, his hands were stuck. It knocked him off balance, and falling forward, his forehead rebounded off the tree's trunk with a hard thunk. Something warm started to run down his face. The contact had split open his forehead, and based on the throbbing, he could tell the gash was directly between his eyebrows.

Blood began to leak into Trevor's eyes and he shook his head to clear his vision. He needed to free his hands. The sheen of red, which distorted his vision, made everything around him dance in a macabre shimmy. He looked down to see that his hands were caught under a large root. The root appeared to be moving, squeezing his hands tighter, holding them in place.

Trevor managed to swipe his face with the shoulder of his shirt, and saw that the roots were simply resting on top of his hands. His hands must have kept trying to remove the root even during the second daydream. But try as he might he couldn't pull his hands out of the dirt. They were stuck on something, but he couldn't figure out what.

A small blossom of panic rose into his chest, but he took a few deep breaths and tried to wiggle his fingers. He was still able to move them a bit, so he started working his hands back and forth, trying to dislodge them.

He leaned over the hole, trying to see through the dark blood invading his eyes. Trevor watched as his hands struggled to free themselves. Now blood dripped down into the hole, and he panicked. His breaths came quicker and a moan escaped his lips.

It was at that moment he heard the whispers. It sounded like the voices of a hundred people, muttering soothsayer words into his ears in an attempt to lull him into a sense of calm.

"Is anyone there?" Trevor asked tentatively.

No response but murmurs.

"Please, somebody help," he tried, a little louder.

Whispers.

An involuntary whimper entered the atmosphere and echoed a hundred times back to him. Tears sprung into Trevor's eyes and he decided to yank his right hand as hard as he could.

Steeling himself for the pain he knew would accompany his decision, Trevor took a few shallow breaths and then pulled on his right hand. The popping sound reached his ears moments before the pain reached his brain. He screamed. Tears splashed on the dirt, dampening the earth around the hole he had dug.

He tried to move the fingers on his right hand, but nothing happened. Either he had dislocated his wrist, or something had snapped. Either way he knew he needed to find a way to escape the root and get to a hospital.

Unfortunately, Trevor had not been paying attention to his breathing and he felt himself become lightheaded. The world began to spin in front of him, vertigo pushing against his senses. He couldn't stop himself from hyperventilating and watched as the world went black and he was carried…

A beeping sound filled the room. Trevor crinkled his brow in confusion. Then the memory of the woods and the tree came crashing in and his eyes flew open, revealing a white, sterile-looking ceiling.

The beeps continued unperturbed, and Trevor hazarded a glance around the room. He was in a hospital room. Someone must have found him in the forest and rescued him. He sighed with relief and a soft sob escaped from deep inside.

He tried to shift his right wrist and found that it moved freely with no pain. So he tried his left hand to make sure it hadn't somehow been left behind. He felt his wrist click, the remnants of an old sports injury, and let out a sobbing *AHA!*

A door opened and a face appeared over him. It was his girlfriend.

Confused, Trevor opened his mouth to speak, but she put a finger to her lips and anothere to his, indicating that he needed to stay silent.

"I came here to say one thing. And then you will never hear from me again. Nod if you understand."

Trevor stared at her for a long moment and then slowly nodded.

"Someone found you in the woods. You had a laceration on your forehead. It looked like someone bludgeoned you with something." His girlfriend paused, taking a deep, shuddering breath to clear her head.

"You were on private property. The owner claims to not know that you were even there, but the police believe he was the only one who could have hit you." She licked her lips.

Trevor opened his mouth again to say something, to inform her that he hit his head on the tree, to let her know everything was all right. But the look on her face made him close it.

She continued, "We are done. We need to end this. All we do is hurt each other."

Trevor lifted his head, but she shook hers and again put her finger to her lips. She would not be deterred from speaking what was on her mind.

"You're not more to blame for our situation than I am. I should have supported you in your decision to try something different. I could have been less suspicious about your enlightenment trip to the beach. But, you closed down. You shut yourself off from the rest of the world. Nothing mattered to you except your stupid projects." She shook her head, emotion tugging at her voice.

"You need to figure out what it is you want, and I need to move on. I tried to wait for you, but you made it impossible. I grabbed all my stuff from the apartment and left the spare key in your kitchen."

As Trevor listened to his girlfriend explain the end of their relationship, he began to feel a strong sense of déjà vu. He had already had this conversation with her. Why was she even at the hospital talking to him about this? The only thought that made any sense was that he had forgotten to remove her as his emergency contact.

He felt his girlfriend grab his hand and squeeze it lightly. She looked directly into his eyes and said, "You are good at building furniture. I never gave you a chance to prove yourself. The coffee table you made is amazing. You could probably sell it for a lot of money."

Trevor remembered the coffee table. It had been his first attempt and he had actually succeeded. He had given it to the woodworker as a thank you for everything he had taught him. Why would his girlfriend think he could sell it? It was already gone. There was no way he could take it back and sell it. That would be a horrible thing to do.

"I know you want to give it to that guy," his girlfriend's voice cut off his thoughts. "But you need to make some money or you won't even have a place to live."

Want to give it to that guy? What guy? There's no other guy to give it to.

His girlfriend must have seen the confusion on his face, because she added, "That woodworker. You said you wanted to give it to him as a thank you."

But, I already did, he thought.

And then he remembered his first trip out to the woods after finishing the coffee table. He had packed his knapsack with so many tools, because he was still experimenting with which of them worked best, and his hammer had fallen out of the pack. He had been looking for that hammer when he felt it smack into his forehead. He didn't know who had done it, never saw the person's face, but he remembered waking up in the hospital.

This wasn't now. This was before. This was when his girlfriend broke up with him. She was about to walk out of his life forever and there was nothing he could do. There was no defending his own actions, or pleading with her to stay, or talking through the relationship with her. Because he remembered that he had stayed completely silent during the entire conversation. He had lain on the bed and listened to everything she had to say and had left it at that. On the inside he could scream how sorry he was at how everything turned out, but the memory was history, and he couldn't change history.

He felt tears leaking out of the sides of his eyes and his girlfriend leaned in, wiped them away, and kissed him goodbye. It was a lingering kiss that was passionate and devastating all at once. Trevor closed his eyes, trying to take a mental snapshot of the moment so he would never forget it.

He opened his eyes and stared out into the forest. The tree he was working on was no longer in front of him. Somehow, he must have gotten his hands free of the root. He tried to move his hands, but nothing happened. After a moment of confusion he tried to move his legs, but they were stuck fast. His head wouldn't turn. The only thing he could move were his eyes, which rolled in their sockets, trying to make sense of what was occurring.

Struggling to change position was doing him no good, so Trevor decided to rest and let his eyes do the work for a while. The trees all around him were as magnificent and majestic as the one he had been focused on, but there were features that seemed a bit off to him.

His vision dulled for a moment, and it felt as though his body were involuntarily moving further away from the trees. And in that moment, he thought he could make out shapes in the bark of the other trees. He knew people who were able to anthropomorphize inanimate objects as if they had faces emblazoned on their surfaces. Pareidolia, he was pretty sure it was called. But he had never had that gift of sight.

However, as his eyes scanned the other trees around him he thought he could make out an ear on one, a mouth on another, a whole face staring directly back at him. He tried to laugh, but it came out sounding creaky and weak.

His vision dulled a second time, and it seemed as though a thin film was placed in front of his eyes. He couldn't quite see as clearly as he had before. A deep fatigue set into his bones, and he thought he might close his eyes for a bit. Maybe after a short rest he would be able to move again and go home. Not every venture into the forest was successful, and he would simply have to chalk this one up as one of those.

A set of eyes hiding just beneath the surface of a birch tree directly opposite where he was suddenly moved. Trevor tried to inhale, but everything hurt. The pain emanated from his chest outward, almost a crushing sensation. Another wave of exhaustion passed over him and he closed his eyes for a moment. When he opened them again no eyes were moving, and if he could have laughed he would have let loose, telling the world that the rope of his sanity was nearly completely frayed.

He was so tired though. And it hurt to try and move or speak or even breathe. Claustrophobia hit him and in a last-ditch effort, he attempted to escape whatever was holding him in one place. Something wrapped around him tighter, constricting his breathing, a burst of stars appearing before his eyes.

Maybe I'll go to sleep for a bit, he thought. *Rest up to regain my strength.* And that's what he did. He closed his eyes, listening to the whispers of the forest. They lulled him into a deep, restful slumber. And he slept.

THE DEAD OF NIGHT

1

Charlie Davidson stepped out of the cabin after his first night in the forest and sighed. He had accepted a ludicrous seasonal position for ludicrous seasonal pay and was feeling quite all right about it. There had been a Job-Hunter ad, which normally he would ignore if he weren't feeling so desperate, and he had clicked on it and started perusing the various listings. Most of the jobs seemed fake or were way out of his ability range.

After nearly an hour of scrolling and putting in for only two job offerings he was about to give up and hit the streets again. He went to click out of the tab but accidentally opened one last posting. It was a seasonal position (winter) that paid really well ($50,000), but there wasn't much of a job description. Charlie told himself that this was again one of those too-good-to-be-true scams, but he hit 'apply' anyway.

He stood up from his desk and heard his phone ding. Looking at it he realized that the people from the posting had already responded. That sent a big red flag into the sky, but Charlie honestly had nothing better to do, so he replied, and an interview was set for the next day.

The interview went smoothly, although he noticed there were some odd questions like, 'If you saw a duck crossing the road, would you stop to let it pass, or would you try and swerve around and continue on your way?' and 'Are you pure of heart?' When Charlie really stopped to think about it, the first question could pertain to being an ad-hoc forest ranger, but the second one bugged him. He figured they were simply asking about integrity.

He walked away from the interview with a job and the promise of $5,000 to be direct deposited to his account before he started work. The $5,000 was for supplies and anything else he might need during his time in the woods. It would not be taken out of his guaranteed pay.

They did warn him that the cabin itself was situated about 30 miles down a forest road that nobody really ever used unless they were up to no good, so he needed to be prepared to deal with the isolation. He said it wasn't a problem, made a lame joke about being a loner, and shook their hands.

The interviewers explained that his main job would be to keep any ne'er do wells out of the forest. Teens and young adults liked to go out deep into the woods and party and leave behind as much paraphernalia/trash as they could. They explained that there would be an ATV waiting for him at the cabin that he would be able to drive around to make the job super easy, and that part of his work was to safely spot any traps that might endanger the local wildlife. The last bit of instruction he received was to make sure he was back at the cabin before night fell. Getting lost in the woods was not recommended, and very easy to happen.

As he stood on the porch of the cabin, breathing in the freshest air he had ever encountered, he felt like this would be a great boost to help him with future jobs. *Heck*, he thought, *maybe I'll do such a bang-up job that they'll want to hire me full time.* And with that idea rattling around in his brain he set off to the shed to check on the ATV.

Sure enough, an ATV that looked almost new was waiting for him. The keys were in the ignition, but when he tried to start it, it clicked twice and went silent. He thought maybe the battery was dead, but then he saw two batteries sitting on a shelf and realized he was meant to install a battery himself. The interviewers had warned him there would be no wi-fi this deep in the forest, so he couldn't even go online and watch a tutorial on how to properly install an ATV battery. He made a mental note to call and ask about that little conundrum later in the day.

A quick search of the shed revealed some gardening tools, a large pile of flower bulbs, and a can half filled with gasoline. It would probably be a good idea to drive into town and pick up more. The gas in the can was probably too old to use anyway.

Glancing at his watch he decided it was as good a time as any to get to walking. He had about three hours before he needed to eat lunch, which would give him a little time to familiarize himself with his surroundings. Luckily, he had downloaded a map app that allowed him to snapshot the area he would be watching, marking his starting point so he didn't get lost. He had had to pay the extra money in order to make the map available offline, but he felt that fifty bucks out of his initial pay was a small price. It would also give him a fairly accurate reading on miles he walked, steps he needed to jumpstart his fitness hopes.

As he hiked the trails, pushing deeper into the park, he had time to ruminate on why someone would pay him $50,000 for three months of work instead of hiring an actual park ranger. And why hadn't they told him about the ATV needing to be re-batteried. This in turn got him wondering if the phone in the cabin even worked. He wasn't excited about the prospect of having to drive into town already. But if he was going to download a tutorial to help him, it seemed like his only choice. The ATV would certainly save him from walking hundreds of acres of land. Besides, picking up more gas for the vehicle was probably a wise move too.

Looking at his phone he saw it was already almost noon, so he followed the squiggly line back to its origin point, the cabin. Surprisingly, it was less than a mile away. Somehow, without realizing, he had looped back toward his new accomodations.

When he arrived back at the cabin, he went inside, washed up, made a sandwich, and then hopped in his car.

2

Mossy Rock was a smallish town, but at least it had the internet. Within five minutes of returning to civilization, Charlie had downloaded five tutorials (just in case) and bought two gas cans that he filled and put in the back of his car. Since he was in town he decided to explore a little and found a quaint antique and oddities shop that looked fun.

The proprietor was nowhere to be found when he entered the building, but Charlie was instantly mesmerized by the trinkets on display. There were crosses, bracelets, charms, necklaces, statues, books, you name it.

He was about to leave when he heard a back door open and looked up to see a gentleman in his late sixties staring at him.

"Hello young fellow, what brings you into my store today?" There was a twinkle in his eye. Charlie imagined this place was a passion of his.

"Well, I don't know if you've heard, but I'm the new guy out in the forest about 30 miles from here," Charlie replied.

He watched the man's countenance falter for a moment, but he recovered just as quickly. "Well, isn't that nice? Anything I can do for you in here? Anything catch your fancy?"

Charlie shook his head. "Just looking, I guess. You have a lot of cool stuff in here." He walked over to a display case and saw what appeared to be a dark leather-bound book. It was unlike anything he had ever seen before.

"What's this?" Charlie asked, pointing to the book.

The old man walked over and looked at it, confused. "Well, I don't know what this is doing out here. That's supposed to be in the archives room in the back. Must've been in a hurry the other day and just shoved it in here." He pulled out a metal ring overstuffed with keys, but found the one he was looking for on his first try. Grabbing the book and shutting the case he smiled apologetically at Charlie.

"I'm gonna go put this in the back right quick. Be out in a jiffy."

And just like that he was gone. Charlie continued to wander the store, not wanting to simply leave without saying anything more.

Nearly five minutes later the old man reappeared and approached Charlie. "Sorry again about that. Looking at the crosses, I see?"

Charlie nodded. "Yeah, there are some really cool designs on some of these."

"Which one is your favorite?" the old man asked, the twinkle returning to his eye.

Charlie pursed his lips and squinted his eyes and finally settled on a cross that looked like ebony twigs intertwined to create the shape. "This one right here. What is that, ebony?"

The old man smiled warmly. "You've got a keen eye, young fella. Tell you what, as an apology why don't you take it?"

Immediately Charlie shook his head. "No, I couldn't do that. It looks expensive."

"Pish-posh," the old man said and pulled his vast key ring out again. And, again, he found the correct one on the first try. "I've been running this place for the last 50 years. I don't think one little old cross is going to dip me into the river of poverty."

Charlie was taken aback. "Thank you. It's beautiful. I look forward to seeing it every day while I'm out in that forest."

The mention of the forest brought the cloud over the old man's eyes once again.

It was noticeable enough that Charlie felt he should ask a question. "Am I the first person that's been hired for this position?"

The old man bit the inside of his lip and slightly shook his head. "Same people have hired a winter caretaker for as long as I can remember."

"They ever hire the same person twice?" Charlie asked with a wink.

"Can't say they have."

The old man suddenly looked very tired, so Charlie decided it was time to thank him and be on his merry way.

As he approached the door he turned one last time and asked, "What was that book anyway?"

There were a few moments where Charlie could see the man struggling internally with some sort of decision, but then he said, "It's called a grimoire." That shadow again. Then, "But it's not for you."

He said the last with a hint of menace, and Charlie took that as his cue to head out.

As he was walking through the door he heard the old man call out to him one last time, "Best to get back to the cabin before dark. Those roads can be tricky."

"All right. Thank you," Charlie called over his shoulder.

3

The next few days were fairly uneventful. He managed to get the ATV up and running, only shocking himself twice in the process. He was thrilled with this, because his legs were almost jelly after the first day he had walked the forest. Plus, he could cover an exponentially larger area every day now.

While he ate lunch he opened his map app and created seven zones, one for each day of the week. He didn't know if he would physically be able to patrol all that space, but he was going to give it his best try. If he had to adjust the zones later, he would adjust the zones later.

Walking out to the ATV he could feel a drop in temperature. He expected it to happen, the skies were clear and the air crisp. He had some time before the first snow. Zipping up his snow jacket, he settled onto the ATV, and started patrolling his first zone. He made sure to always carry a large black garbage bag (which he had gotten in town) and one of those grabby dealies (which he also had gotten in town). Even though he was miles and miles from civilization there was still trash to be found.

As he drove around, Charlie began to fantasize about what he could do with the money and soon became depressed. All his fantasies involved paying off this bill or that bill. And soon, using the calculator in his brain, he was broke again. But he felt confident that he could at least pay everything off and start from scratch instead of in a hole.

He had gotten so lost in his own head that he hadn't noticed the sun sinking below the horizon. Suddenly it was dusk, and he was a few miles out from his cabin. Remembering the admonition to not be out after dark, and noticing his phone only had 8% battery life, he immediately turned and headed back home.

The last rays of sunlight were filtering through the trees as he parked the ATV and opened the door to the cabin. It was then that he thought he heard a large animal somewhere behind him. Years of running up stairs quickly, not dangling his arms or legs over the sides of beds, and fastidiously locking doors kicked in and he panicked. He slammed the door behind him and then pressed his ear up to it to listen.

He heard nothing, took a deep breath, laughed nervously to himself and went into the kitchen to make dinner. That is when he heard it; a snuffling sound. It was coming from directly outside his front door. There were windows to either side of the door and he quietly shifted his position so he could look out and catch a glimpse of whatever animal had made its way up onto his porch.

It was already pitch dark outside, but he thought he could make out a hunched over figure in the shadows. He stared intently, waiting for his eyes to adjust to the darkness, but before they could it was gone. Perhaps it was only imagination playing tricks. Maybe there had been nothing there. But just in case, he double checked the door to make sure the lock was properly bolted and laughed at himself. To calm and distract himself, he decided that after supper he would watch one of the movies he had downloaded on his phone. And then maybe another, for good measure.

4

The next morning Charlie woke up to three inches of snow. And the snow continued to fall. He had never been more grateful for the ATV.

Now, he had the opportunity to fully gear up in his winter attire, and after bundling as best he could he noticed the clothing was a little loose. He hadn't realized that he had been losing any weight, but he took it as a positive sign that his walks were paying off.

He got to the ATV, turned it on, backed it out of the shed, and set an alarm on his phone for 3:30pm so he didn't run into the same problem he had the day before. It would be dark by 4:30pm this time of year thanks to Daylight Saving.

The day passed quickly. Around noon he pulled out his lunchbox and ate a sandwich, some chips and drank an energy drink he had packed. The snow hadn't let up and he watched it slowly pile up, reaching six inches by the time he finished eating. It was absolutely beautiful. Here was a spot on earth that hadn't been spoiled by humans other than some trails, and the occasional pile of litter. It was such a rarity anymore, with humanity's innate desire to know and then use everything. A thought passed through his mind. No one should know about this place. They would turn it into a tourist attraction and then everything would be ruined. He vowed to never talk about how breathtaking or awe-inspiring it was. 'It was all right' should suffice.

He had nearly filled his trash bag by the time his alarm went off on his phone. Checking to see how far he was from the cabin (6 miles), he decided to call it a day and head back.

Charlie allowed himself to enjoy the feel of the snowflakes as they zipped past him, some of them making contact and slowly melting on his face. He imagined he could do this permanently. If they hired someone for every season he could make $200k a year. Surprisingly, he hadn't even noticed the lack of internet connection. In fact, he felt refreshed not doomscrolling through the inane thoughts people posted for the world to see. Nothing was original. Nothing was important. It was simply a way to say, 'Hey, look at me. I'm important. Tell me I'm important.' It was all rather sad.

He arrived back at the cabin with plenty of time to spare, so he cleaned up the shed a little and pulled a steak out of the freezer to thaw for dinner. Charlie was beginning to feel something he had never anticipated in his life. It took him a minute to realize what it was, but when he did he nodded his head and whispered, "I'm content."

That's when the knock came. A solid three knocks on the front door that startled Charlie. He looked at the windows on either side of the door and found that it was pure dark again outside.

A million thoughts ran through Charlie's head: *Who could be out here? How did they find the cabin? Are they hurt? Are they in trouble?* On and on they swirled through his mind. He almost decided to shut off his lights and act like he hadn't heard the knocking, but then it happened again, so he took a deep breath and walked up to the door.

Opening it, he saw a figure in a cloak, the face obscured by the shadows, standing in the constant snowfall. It didn't say anything, as if waiting for Charlie to break the silence.

Finally, he did, "Are you all right?"

The figure shook its head.

"How did you find your way here?"

The figure shrugged its shoulders.

"If you need help, you need to tell me what is wrong."

A long silence, and then, "May I come in?"

Alarm bells sounded in Charlie's head. This is how he was going to be killed. Somehow a murderer had found their way to the middle of the forest, and they were going to stab him to death, leaving the corpse as a warning to others.

Charlie started to close the door. "I'm sorry, but no. I can see that you are in a bit of distress, but I don't feel comfortable letting you into my house."

He thought he heard a low hissing sound, but then the figure said, "Please. I just need to use your telephone."

"I can make a phone call for you," Charlie said, shaking his head.

The figure stood for another minute in silence and then stated, "Don't worry about it. I'll try to find my own way out of the forest."

Charlie didn't know what to say, and he surprised himself when he heard his mouth utter the word, "Okay," to the stranger.

Apparently it took the stranger by surprise as well, because Charlie watched the cowl covering his face twitch to the side.

"Tell you what," Charlie began. "I will go inside and call the police so they can come out and escort you safely back into town. That way you aren't out there freezing to death. Does that sound good?"

The cowl shook back and forth. No.

"Well, I don't know what to tell you. I can't let you in, because I'm afraid." Charlie figured honesty was the best policy here.

The man, if it was a man, looked toward the telephone and pointed, "Just let me make the call real quick." And when he turned back to the figure, it was gone. Charlie couldn't even make out any footprints in the snow.

Charlie knew it would be another night of downloaded movies for him. He shut the door, locked and chained it, put the coffee table in front of it, even though logically he thought, *Duh, they could just break one of the many windows that surrounded the cabin.*

He tried to put it out of his head as best he could and made his way into the kitchen to cook his steak.

5

When Charlie woke up from a restless sleep, he couldn't shake the encounter he had had the night before. It seemed very odd that a person would be all the way out here but refuse help from the authorities. In fact, the figure had almost seemed disappointed that Charlie had not allowed him inside.

Throughout the day, at the most random times, he would remember the figure and shudder. It was unnerving. Yet, there was nothing he could do about it unless he decided to head back into town and ask around about a vagrant wandering in the woods. He imagined he might still do that when he made his next journey to civilization, but that wouldn't be for a few more days. He still had half a container of gas for the ATV and plenty of food.

Mid-afternoon came and Charlie found it increasingly difficult to concentrate on his work. His garbage bag was half full, and he decided to call it early for once. It wasn't like he was doing a crap job or anything. The irrational part of his brain told him this would be the time something would go haywire in the forest, and he would miss it and get in trouble. But he told himself that could be happening every night after dark, and the internal argument seemed to be resolved.

Afternoon turned into evening turned into night, and as Charlie was preparing to bed down he heard the three sharp knocks at his door again. This time terror flooded his body with adrenaline, and he grabbed a knife from the kitchen and approached the door. He leaned his head against it and said, "Please go away."

He heard the shuffling of feet and then a soft reply, "Please, just let me in."

"Why?" Charlie heard himself ask.

"Everyone before you has," came the reply.

A chill shot straight up Charlie's spine. "And what happened to them?"

A soft chuckle and then, "If I told you that you probably would never let me in."

Another chill. "Well, then it seems that it's going to be a hard no forever."

The figure banged on the door with both fists and Charlie heard footsteps walking away.

There was a long silence, and he hazarded a glance out of one of the windows, but he couldn't see anything. Then he heard a sniff.

Feeling bold for whatever reason he cracked one of the windows and tentatively asked, "You still there?"

Nothing. Then, "Yeah. I'm still here."

Charlie bit the inside of his cheek and then asked, "So the plan is to kill me then?"

"Eh," was all he got back.

"Why didn't you just barge your way in yesterday? What are you, a vampire?" Charlie laughed at his own joke.

Silence.

"Wait, no. Vampires aren't real. You're messing with me." Charlie weakly laughed again, this time with a hint of fear mixed in.

"My name is Peter," he stated.

"And you're a vampire," Charlie whispered.

"And I'm a vampire," Peter confirmed.

Charlie slid down the wall until he was sitting below the still open window. He felt comfortable doing this, even though his thoughts were screaming at him that this was all a ploy to let his guard down.

"And that's why you can't come in without permission." If any of this was true, this was a relief.

"Correct. Now, can you please let me in?"

"Hell no!"

"So, you are fine with letting me starve simply because you don't want to die? Seems a bit selfish," Peter responded tartly.

"But you don't have an accent. Aren't vampires supposed to have accents? You know, 'I vant to suck your bloodt' that kind of thing?

Charlie heard what sounded like Peter banging his head against the wall. "Hollywood really has done a number hasn't it? I'm from America. I've only been a vampire for a little over 400 years. You know your history?"

"Enough," replied Charlie.

"Heard of Roanoke?"

"That's the place where everyone disappeared, yeah?"

"Tada!" Charlie imagined he could see Peter raising his arms as if in a reveal.

"So, everyone in Roanoke…" he found he couldn't finish the question.

"Eaten or turned," Peter confirmed.

"So, I've got a question." Charlie held his breath, waiting an invitation, but when it didn't come he asked, "What does Croatoan mean?"

"I have no idea what that word is," Peter replied.

"Really?"

"No, I'm just messing with you."

"You are a sassy vampire, aren't you?"

"When you've been alive for as long as I have it kind of comes with the territory." Charlie imagined the shrug of Peter's shoulders.

"Do you mind me asking these questions? I'm sure you've answered them all a million times over," Charlie said.

Peter thought for a moment and then responded, "Actually, most people I encounter let me right in and our business is conducted very quickly. Not often is there time for questions."

"I guess that makes sense," Charlie replied.

"So, you're gonna let me in, right?" Peter persisted.

"Hell no."

Silence. Then, "Fine."

Charlie licked his lips and tentatively said, "But we can keep talking. I'm okay with talking."

A long silence. Charlie lifted his eyes to the window, sure he had lost his conversation partner, but then he heard a sigh and a mutter. "I guess so."

"My name's Charlie, by the way."

"Charlie, nice to meet you. And I apologize."

"For what? Wanting to eat me?"

"I don't eat people. I'm not a zombie."

Charlie thought about it for a second. "Fair."

"No, I apologize for slashing all your tires on your car," came the timid reply.

Charlie bolted to his feet and futilely tried to check on his car. It was pitch black still. "You did what?! When did you do that?"

"Yesterday. I was sure you would have noticed by now, but I guess not."

Charlie choked on his spit. "But… well, I don't drive it every day."

"Also…" Peter began.

"Also? Did you smash my engine?"

"No, nothing like that. Of course not." A long silence and then very quickly, "I slashed the tires on your ATV as well."

"Dammit, Peter!" Charlie yelled at him.

"What do you expect? I was supposed to make it look like things went wrong and you wandered into the forest trying to find your way to town and got lost."

Charlie stopped at that. He blinked a couple times and then said, "What do you mean, you were supposed to make it look like things went wrong?"

All Charlie could hear for the longest time was Peter adjusting his position on the porch. Finally, "Promise you won't be mad?"

This set Charlie off. "Mad? I'm furious! It's too late for all that. You come here, try to suck my blood, slash all of the tires, and then casually mention that this was all part of the plan?"

There was no reply, so Charlie finished with, "You bet your ass I'm mad. So you might as well tell me."

Nothing for a long time. Peter sat quietly on one side of the wall and Charlie paced angrily on the other.

After what felt like an eternity Peter finally spoke. "The people that employed you, did they ask you any strange questions? Like, are you pure of heart?"

This caused Charlie to stop pacing. "Yeah. They did ask me that."

"The reason they asked you that is because there is a difference in the quality of sustenance between someone pure of heart and someone…well… not-so-pure of heart."

"Go on."

"If I am able to feed on someone who has a pure heart it can sustain me for an entire season. That's why they send someone out every season."

"To die?"

"To die."

"And how many not pure hearts would you have to feed on in order to sustain you for a season?" Charlie asked with a lump in his throat.

"I haven't reached a number yet," came the reply.

"What's the most you've fed on then?"

"Fifty?" Peter phrased it more as a question.

"That's messed up," Charlie said matter-of-factly.

"I don't disagree," Peter said. "So, the people that hired you get a grant every quarter for $5,000, which they pay in advance to their new forest caretaker, knowing full well they will never have to pay out the full amount at the end of the season."

"Phew," was all Charlie could think to say.

"If you think about it, they are doing a great service for the locals. I live out here and help protect the forest and they provide me with a meal, so I don't go into town and feed on who knows how many people in order to survive."

Charlie didn't know what to say to that. All he knew was that he would continue to deny this vampire entry into his home so that he could live. All he had to do was last the season and then he could get out of there with a big payday. But that made him think of some problems he would face, the most important being the lack of food.

"Thirty miles into town. That means I couldn't make it during daylight hours, because there's maybe 10 hours of daylight right now. Can you promise me if I try to make it to town that you would leave me alone?" Charlie asked hopefully.

"There's no way. When the hunger takes over I don't have the ability to stop it. Take right now for instance. If you were to say I could come in—"

"Not a chance," Charlie blurted.

"If being the operative word here. If you were to say I could come in then it would all be over moments later."

"That sucks," Charlie said without thinking.

"Ha ha," Peter laughed sardonically.

"Sorry. That was unintentional," Charlie said with absolute sincerity.

He looked at his watch and saw that it was midnight already. "Peter, I hate to cut our time short, but thanks for chatting."

Another long silence and then, "Can I come back tomorrow?"

"Are you going to ask me if you can come in?"

"Every time," Peter replied.

Charlie thought for a long minute and then responded, "See you tomorrow night."

"Tomorrow night then. Goodnight, Charlie."

"Goodnight, Peter."

Charlie heard Peter saunter off into the darkness and then he sat heavily on the couch. *There's no way Peter is a vampire*, he thought to himself. *He's just messing around with me. I'm still not going to let him in, but there's no way he's a vampire.*

Right?

6

The next evening Charlie was making his dinner when he heard the familiar three knocks on the door, but instead of opening the door he opened the window. Looking down he could just see the silhouette of Peter sitting on the porch leaning against the wall.

"Hello again," Charlie said.

"Hey, I've got an idea. Why don't you let me in so we can be properly introduced," Peter said as if the idea had just occurred to him.

"I'm gonna have to say no to that," Charlie replied.

"Figures," Peter said, pretending to feel dejected. "What do you want to talk about tonight?"

"I've been thinking all day about you being a vampire and I of course have the top ten questions of all time that I am hoping to ask."

Peter sighed, "Let me save you some time. No, vampires cannot turn into bats. Bram started that ridiculousness when he wrote *Dracula*. On that note, yes Dracula was inspired by Vlad the Impaler, but Vlad had a whole other set of problems, none of which were vampirism. Garlic is gross, but it doesn't repel vampires any more than regular humans. Let's see. What else. The process of becoming a vampire breaks down the stratum corneum that is present on every human epidermis and is how we are protected from the UV rays of the sun. Without that protection the sun literally creates a sunburn so intense that it can burst into flames. So, that's a very real threat. Even at dusk there is a risk involved."

Charlie looked up and saw the ebony cross he was given at the little shop in Mossy Rock. "What about crosses? Do they actually repel vampires?"

"Sometimes," came the quick reply.

"Why only sometimes?"

"That's a tricky one, because I actually don't know. There have been times when I approached a person and learned, after I had drained them, they were wearing a cross around their neck. It had no effect on me whatsoever. Then there are other times where if I step into a room and a cross is even in the same area I can feel it affecting me. Best I can guess is that I have stepped onto holy ground."

"So, holy ground is a real thing?"

Charlie could feel Peter nodding his head. "Oh yes. But not in the way you might imagine. Everyone has always interpreted holy ground as a space that has been sanctified, usually with holy water, the blood of Christ, etc. But holy ground is in the heart of an individual. It's the person that makes the area around them holy. The cross is simply a physical totem of that holiness."

Charlie laughed. "So churches must be a nightmare, huh?"

"Charlie, there is a big difference between being holy and being sanctimonious. Fortunately for us vampires most churches are not holy places. So, I mean, if you want to know a good church to attend, take me with you and I can be your divining rod."

Charlie furrowed his brow and asked, "If you can't be near a cross that is associated with a holy person, how come the person themselves don't repel you?"

An even thicker darkness fell over the porch, and it took a while for Peter to respond. "This is why someone who is holy, pure of heart, what have you, can sustain us for so long. You know how penicillin is made, yes? A penicillium mold is grown and then the penicillin is extracted and purified to make the vaccination. If you were to stand around the mold without any protective gear you would eventually get sick and possibly die. But extracting and purifying the penicillin creates an antibody that helps you."

"So, the holiness of a person is essential to a vampire's survival, but if not done properly it can kill you," Charlie responded quietly.

"Everyone has holiness inside them. In varying levels, of course. Draining for some, is like sticking your head into a clear mountain stream and opening your mouth, but with others it's like trying to suck the moisture out of a handkerchief. That's why your employer sends out those who are pure of heart. It's almost a wash to drain someone whose holiness has been nearly forgotten. But for someone who lives in the truth of their being, which is holy, draining them feels like being well rested for the first time in centuries. There is pleasure and there is pain associated with draining humans."

Charlie didn't know how to respond. The idea that the best among humanity were the ones that were needed to allow a twisted creature to continue existing seemed unfair.

As if reading his mind, Peter said, "Life isn't fair. Especially when it comes to this symbiosis.

When Charlie spoke it was very quietly, "I don't think I can do this anymore tonight. Can you come back tomorrow?"

There was no response. Instead, Charlie heard Peter stand up and walk away.

7

When Charlie opened his eyes the next morning he felt like something within him had shifted. The concepts Peter had talked about the night before sat heavy on his mind. He felt like he was being re-educated. It was as though he were a baby learning to walk. There was too much to comprehend. And yet he still had questions. Some of them felt silly after how deep the conversation had gone, but he felt like he needed to ask them.

Maybe Peter wouldn't return. Maybe after last night he would recognize how horribly sick this relationship was. But deep-down Charlie knew that wasn't true. Peter needed to feed, and Charlie was the only one out here that could fulfill that necessity.

Peter did return that evening. Same knock on the door. Same refusal to be let inside. And they talked until midnight about friends lost and times they felt wanted and unwanted. Charlie wanted to ask more questions about Peter the vampire, but by the time he would have gotten around to it, it was time for sleep.

Charlie stood up and stretched. Looking through the window he could see Peter looking in at him. He sensed the hunger emanating through the empty frame. But fear didn't accompany the fact that there was only air between him and this vampire. Peter offered him a sad smile and turned to leave, when Charlie thought of one last question he wanted to ask and cleared his throat.

"I know sometimes vampires are said to be able to enter people's dreams. Is that another Hollywood myth?"

Peter stopped and thought about it for a while and then nodded his head. "I've never tried, but I'm pretty sure without using a glammer on someone there is no way for me to get into your head."

Charlie smiled and went to shut the window. Right before the pane whispered shut, he heard Peter say, "But if you dream about me, let me know."

And then he was off into the night, and Charlie was off to bed. He had no dreams that night.

8

Over the next month Peter came every night to talk. Charlie would make sure he was inside before dusk, and then stoke the fire so he wouldn't freeze while chatting. Their conversations ranged from favorite movies to favorite books to trading aphorisms.

Charlie started writing down questions he wanted to ask Peter, so he wouldn't forget, and every night started the same way:

Peter would knock three times on the door and ask, "Can I come in?"

Charlie would walk up to the window, open it and say, "Hell no."

And then they would sit on either side of the wall talking until midnight.

One night Charlie asked, "Have you ever been in love?"

Peter stayed silent for a long while before answering. If Charlie thought vampires slept at night he would have assumed Peter had dozed off.

He was about to ask again when Peter said, "Once. When I was human."

"In Roanoke?" Charlie asked.

"Yeah. In Roanoke. Her name was Elizabeth. She was the kindest, most lovely person I've ever known."

Charlie could hear the nostalgia and latent pain in Peter's voice, but he stayed silent.

"She was betrothed to another, and by the time I got up the courage to ask her if she might marry me instead of him, the vampires descended. I tried to save her. By the time I got to her she had been drained. In a fury I ran at the vampire that hovered over her body and pushed him away. But she was already gone." Peter took a deep, shuddering breath.

Charlie whispered, "I'm so sorry, Peter."

Peter continued, "You know what the worst part is? I will never know if they intended on turning her. I attacked the vampire before there was even a chance for him to do anything other than drain her. I'll never know if I could have journeyed these last centuries with my love."

They both listened to the whispering of the wind in the trees and the soft pitter-patter of snowflakes adding to the already thickly covered ground. Charlie regretted bringing up the topic, and he wracked his brain trying to think of a way to lighten the mood. Nothing immediately came to mind, so he let the silence stretch.

After what felt like an hour, but was most likely only a few minutes, Peter sighed and said, "Sorry to bring it down so low."

"My fault," was all Charlie could think to say. "Can I ask you another question? Definitely not one about love."

Peter chuckled. "Go for it."

"Wooden stakes, fact or fiction?" Charlie tried to pose the question in a light way, but it rang false.

"They don't have to be wooden; anything that pierces the heart and remains there disrupts the symbiotic nature of vampirism and death. If you found a good piece of rebar it would do the same thing."

"And that kills a vampire?" Charlie asked.

Peter clucked his tongue. "That one's a little vague. Technically it paralyzes a vampire. If someone removes the object from the heart the vampire will return to its former state. So, you would have to stake them and then drag them into the sunshine to finish the job."

"Brutal work," Charlie said.

"Indeed," Peter agreed.

A short silence, followed by Charlie's stomach grumbling, and then, "Peter?"

"Charlie?" Peter responded.

"I'm almost out of food. I've had to ration as it is. I'm not going to survive out here too much longer." Charlie sounded defeated. He had tried not to think about running out of food, but now it was imminent, and he found he was frightened. If he figured correctly, he could go without food for another few weeks, slowly getting weaker and weaker. At least there was plenty of water in the form of snow. He wouldn't dehydrate.

Peter spoke up. "I've been thinking about that. I could try to go into town and steal some food and bring it to you. But that would mean you wouldn't see me for a couple nights. It's safer to stay halfway between here and town for a day so I don't risk a sunburn."

Charlie guffawed at that. "That might be nice."

Peter stood up. "Okay, I will go tomorrow night, and I will try to be back the night after." He turned to leave.

"Could you do me one more favor? Could I send a note with you so someone could come out and get me?" Charlie knew he was begging, but he was too frightened to care.

Peter shook his head. "I can try, but most everyone in town knows the caretakers have made some sort of deal with something out here in the forest. Most imagine it was a deal with the devil, but whatever they tell themselves, none of them like to come out here."

Charlie moved away from the window and wrote a quick note, balled it up, and threw it through the window. Peter picked it up and read it, nodding.

"As much as I want to drain you, I think we're good enough friends at this point to at least try this," Peter said with a wry smile.

"Thank you, Peter," Charlie said.

The vampire smiled back. "No problem. See you in a couple nights."

Then he disappeared into the dark, and Charlie was off to bed, feeling the gnawings of hunger.

9

True to his word, Peter didn't show up the next night, and when Charlie woke up on the second morning his stomach was in rebellion. Cramps doubled him over a couple times, but in anticipation of Peter returning with food, he ate the last of his stores for breakfast.

Feeling slightly better, he put on his snow clothes and started walking aimlessly through the forest to distract himself, his phone long forgotten on his bedside table. As the day drifted by, Charlie began to see signs of human life. Recent signs. There was a campfire still smoldering in a clearing, surrounded by empty beer bottles and wrappers. A little further on he came across a deer that had been shot and left for dead. There was nothing Charlie could do as the deer stared at him, gasping for breath.

"I'm so sorry," he whispered to the deer, and moved away from it.

As he walked, Charlie began to hope he could run across these people. Sure, they were the type of people that would leave a deer suffering in the woods, but on the other hand he had no other way of getting out of the forest without Peter draining him when the sun went down.

He looked for more signs and when he smelled urine he knew someone must be close. Then he heard the shot. It reverberated around him, so he couldn't pinpoint which direction it came from, but a moment later he heard cheering and laughter and headed west in pursuit of the noise. As he walked he was filled with both trepidation and hope. Here was the possibility of escaping, but the sounds of their behavior wasn't instilling confidence.

After a few more minutes, he heard another cheer and saw a brief movement through the trees in front of him. He burst into the clearing and saw four men standing around a campfire, all drinking beer.

Charlie didn't know what to say, so he started with, "Hello gentlemen, how are you this evening?"

He surprised them enough that one of the men dropped his beer bottle, which shattered on the ground. Charlie was torn between his sense of duty (to a fake job, really) and needing a ride home.

One of the men took a giant step in his direction. "Who the hell are you supposed to be?" he slurred.

"I am the caretaker of this forest and I'm going to have to ask you to leave," Charlie said.

Another of the men started to chortle. "Oooohhh, the caretaker of the forest. Calm down there, Lorax." His speech was even more slurred than the first.

"How long do you fellas plan on being out here in the forest?"

The third man lurched forward with a vicious grin on his face. "What's it to ya, Ranger Dick?"

"Listen, I don't want any trouble with you all. I simply wanted to know if I could get a ride back to town. The tires on my car are all—" he stopped, pondering if he really wanted to tell these guys the truth. "—flat," he continued. "And I don't have a way to fix them. So I'm in a bit of a predicament."

Charlie looked around at all of them, and then realized the sun was setting. "Besides the fact that these woods are really dangerous at night. I highly recommend you get out of here."

The fourth man, the one who dropped his beer when Charlie surprised them, said, "Get out of this," and Charlie barely had time to register the high whistling sound before a bottle struck him in the left temple and shattered, lacerating the side of his face and forehead.

Stunned, he moved his hand to his head, pushing the shards of glass further under the skin. He sat on the ground hard and groaned. Everything was doubled. The world didn't look right. It was tinted red. And now the sun was nearly gone.

Charlie watched helplessly as the men approached him, a couple of them looking concerned. But the one who had thrown the bottle was still laughing and asking his friends, "Did you see it? Direct bullseye!"

Consciousness faded and then returned. He heard them talking amongst themselves. "What do we do with him?" "We're out in the middle of nowhere. We leave him here and no one will know." "That's murder." "Not if we don't get caught." "Hey, shit happens. We don't have the resources to carry him out of here. Besides, he's bleeding pretty bad, and it's already dark so—"

Charlie finally succumbed to the darkness and the last thing he heard was, "What the hell is that?"

And then screaming.

10

Charlie woke up when he felt himself being lowered onto his porch. He couldn't open his eyes, but he heard a voice telling him to crawl. Saying he needed to crawl into the cabin now. It took a few seconds for Charlie to remember what had happened, and his eyes shot open. Crouched ten feet away from him was Peter. It was the first time he had actually seen his face, but most of it was still in the shadows. He appeared to be around the same age as Charlie, but he knew better.

There was something red glistening around Peter's mouth and was about to ask the vampire about it, but he vomited. His head burst in pain.

His eyes unfocused, then refocused.

Peter spoke to him again. "Charlie, I need you to crawl into your cabin and fix yourself up."

So, Charlie began to crawl. It was an arduous task even though he had been set down inches from the threshold. He reached out and touched the door. It was shut. Peter couldn't help him open it. He would have to lift himself off the ground and open it.

Somewhere in the back of his mind he could hear Peter encouraging him, telling him he could do it. A moment of confusion struck Charlie, and he thought, *I can do what?*

Then his head cleared, and he remembered he was trying to open the door to his cabin. With his eyes squeezed shut, he slowly felt along the door until he found the knob. He grasped it and rotated it. Nothing happened. Crying now, he channeled all his strength into this one task and turned with all his might, yelling into the night. He heard a click. And then the world was falling again.

"That's it. Almost there," he heard Peter say in another dimension.

A few last pulls and Charlie felt his feet cross the threshold and into the cabin. Once there, he rested a moment before trying to sit up. He leaned against the couch and finally opened his eyes. Peter was crouched just outside the door, concern etched in his face.

Charlie took a few deep breaths, feeling the pain in his head expand and contract with every inhale and exhale. He was amazed that he hadn't passed out again.

It took him a moment to realize that Peter was talking to him.

"Wazzat?" Charlie slurred, and then chuckled as he reminded himself of the guys out in the forest. Then the pressure in his head became unbearable and he moaned and grabbed at his temples.

"I asked you if there was anything I could do," Peter repeated.

"I doubt it," Charlie responded. "I need to get to the medsin cabnet and bandage myself up."

"Why don't you talk to me while you do that. Huh? What do you say, Charlie?" There was a desperate tone in Peter's voice that Charlie didn't like.

"Fine. Fine. Thass something I can do." He felt his speech returning to him little by little.

"Tell me about your family, Charlie," Peter said.

"Mom is dead. Dad is dead. Only child. Not much to tell," Charlie responded curtly.

"I'm sorry to hear that," returned Peter.

Charlie ignored that as he struggled to stand up. He got halfway to his feet and threw up again. Suddenly he looked directly at Peter and said, "I think you're the first real friend I've had in… well, in ever." Tears welled up in Charlie's eyes as he nodded to confirm what he had said was true.

Peter responded, "That's great Charlie. Keep moving. Stay alive."

Charlie saluted Peter. "Yes sir, captain sir. All aboard." The floor beneath him swam as he tried to stand up again.

"Can I tell you something, Peter?" Peter nodded his head and Charlie continued, "I need to tell you something important. I don't care if you're a vampire. And I don't care that we just met a month ago. I love you. You could have drained me all the way here, but you saved me." The words caught in Charlie's throat as another wave of emotion hit him. "Why did you save me, Peter?"

Charlie looked up and saw deep emotion in Peter's eyes. He didn't think vampires could cry, but if they could he thought that's what Peter would be doing.

"Going through existence for such a long time means watching your loved ones die time and time again. It means watching your adopted children become parents and grandparents and then attending their funerals while you remain young. Eventually the pain becomes unbearable. It is easier to become the heartless killing machine that vampires are usually made out to be. If you are never close to anyone you can never have your heart ripped out."

Peter put his head in his hands. "But then you surprised me. You wouldn't let me into the cabin. It wasn't even a thought that entered your head. And I didn't know what to do with that information." Suddenly he stood up straight and yelled, "Charlie! I need you to stay with me here!"

Charlie had been slowly slumping to one side against the kitchen counter, his eyes becoming unfocused. He lifted his head and smiled as if to say, *A-OK boss.*

"It was intriguing. Nothing has fascinated me in ages. The mundanity of existence took over every aspect of my waking time."

"Why not end it?" Charlie asked, eyes closed, jaw clenched.

"I want to survive. I don't want to give in. I don't want to succumb to the siren call of true death. I'm scared of what comes next. At least humans have possibilities of life after death. But how does that work with vampires? There is nothing in any book that gives a clue as to what happens after a vampire dies. It makes sense. Most people believe vampires are a myth. So, why would they write about the eternal soul of a mythical creature? Huh?"

Peter was silent and Charlie finally stood up to his full height. He looked directly at Peter with tears streaming down his face and said, "I want to believe that you will enjoy or endure the same fate as everyone else. You are still human. You were born a human, and I don't think anything beyond that changes a damn thing. At the core of your being there is nothing wrong with you. Nature takes its course."

Charlie swayed where he stood and Peter nearly stepped over the threshold but held back.

"Charlie, you reminded me that connection is important. I have been so disconnected for so long that I forgot what it felt like. I love you too, Charlie. And I don't want you to die."

Charlie giggled in his stupor. "You sure are saying my name an awful lot," and that being said he collapsed to the ground, convulsions racking his body.

Faintly he could hear Peter yelling at him, but it took him a moment to decipher what he was saying. His body calmed down and he lay on the floor, exhausted.

"You have to invite me in, Charlie! Now! If you don't you'll die!" Peter yelled.

Charlie felt his mouth moving, but no words would come out.

"I have to get you to town now. The ones I drained earlier will help keep my hunger at bay, but it won't be that way forever. We need to go. Night is almost gone as it is. Invite me in. Let me come in."

Charlie opened his mouth again, but all that came out was a small squeak.

Peter was now pacing back and forth on the porch and suddenly he stopped and said, "All I need you to do is nod. I'll ask the question, you nod."

Peter waited for some kind of confirmation, but Charlie's eyes were closed, and he was breathing rapidly.

After a few seconds Peter decided to ask the question, "Charlie, do you give me permission to enter your home?"

Charlie raised an eyebrow.

Peter growled in frustration. "That's not good enough. I need a full head nod. Charlie, do you give me permission to enter your house?"

Charlie smacked his lips together and opened his eyes briefly. Peter saw death waiting behind those eyes and slammed his fists into the siding of the cabin.

Emotion tore through Peter as he tried one last time, afraid that it was already too late. "Nod your head. God damn you, nod your head! Charlie, do you give me permission to enter your house?"

And then he waited. He watched Charlie's eyelids swim up and down threatening to close for good. Then he saw Charlie's lips move, and barely above a whisper he said, "Come in." Peter was inside in a heartbeat and picking Charlie up.

He ran out the front door as fast as he could, encouraging his friend to stay with him.

Charlie felt the breeze on his face and opened his eyes enough to see the trees swiftly moving above him. He had enough time to register how fast he must be moving before he passed out again.

Peter kept running, trying to will Charlie to hold on. He cursed the world for being a cruel place. There was nothing else he could think to do.

There was a sudden shift in visibility and Peter realized the sun was getting ready to come up. He knew he wasn't close to town yet and he let out a bellow of rage. Dropping to his knees he leaned his head on Charlie's chest.

Charlie looked up at Peter and smiled. "It's okay. You tried. You did all you could. Let me give you strength in my last moments. Let me feed you."

Peter was shaking his head, dry sobs convulsing his body.

Charlie reached a hand up and caressed Peter's face. "I give you permission."

The words broke Peter, and he collapsed to the ground. Light was creeping over the ground. He had to make his decision now.

He laid Charlie on the ground and bent over him. A moment later his fangs entered Charlie's jugular, and he drank deep from him. Charlie felt his life leaving his body and when Peter tried to pull away he held him steady against his neck. "Take all you need," he whispered.

And then it was finished. Charlie knew he was fading. He accepted his fate.

And then he heard, "Charlie, I am so sorry. I can't lose you. I hope you can forgive me." Charlie felt warm liquid flow between his lips. And he drank.

WITH A WHIMPER

Snow flurried down, slowly softening the details of the landscape. It had been falling steadily for the better part of three days, but Ranger wasn't deterred. He followed the disappearing tracks into the forest, hoping to surprise his quarry. The sneaky devil had evaded him twice during this extended hunt, and the hunger pangs were affecting his ability to function.

Ranger stepped up to the tree line and closed his eyes, listening for any sound of rustling. All he heard was the muffled sound of snowflakes adding themselves to the inches covering the ground. Taking a deep breath and expelling it forcefully, he stepped into the woods. The soft crunch from his waterproof boots sounded much louder in the infinite silence surrounding him. His shoulders dropped, fatigue pulling at his cognition; he knew if he stopped here he would never start back up. So, he pushed himself to take one step and then another, focusing on each footfall, until finally he peeked back the way he had come and found he could no longer see the edge of the forest.

A whisper of a sound reached his ears, and he held his breath. The noise was slight, a bunny perhaps, or a rodent of some kind. He stood motionless for nearly two minutes before deciding to move on.

He heard the crack of the rifle at the same time a chunk of the tree nearest him splintered, showering him with fragments of wood. Luckily the balaclava took the brunt of the splinters, but a few had sprayed his face below the eyes. In a flash he jumped behind the tree and yelled out,

"Friendly!"

Silence.

Ranger hardly dared breathe, but his eyes moved, roaming from left to right in an attempt to catch anyone trying to sneak up.

He heard a rifle being cocked, and it sounded like it was on the other side of the tree.

"I said friendly," Ranger nearly whispered.

A scoffing sound and then, "Yeah? And how do I know that?"

Ranger didn't have a reply.

"This is my property." The voice sounded tired, like the man hadn't gotten an opportunity to rest since everything fell apart.

"I didn't know this was someone's land. I'll leave," Ranger replied. Then he added, "If you'll let me."

A long silence followed by a muffled coughing fit. "You deputized?"

"Solo hunter," Ranger said.

"Man or beast?"

"Beast. Never man."

Another stretch of silence.

Ranger broke it this time, "My arrows are stowed. I have a three-inch knife in my boot. No gun."

"Throw 'em to the ground."

Ranger did as he was asked.

"Clothes too."

"Why?" Ranger asked, perturbed at the request.

"Need to make sure you ain't hiding anything else." Again, a fit of coughing broke through the stillness.

With a frustrated sigh, Ranger acquiesced and threw his clothes on top of his bow and arrow and knife.

"Hands."

Very slowly Ranger maneuvered his hands around the trunk of the tree. The bitter cold hit him like a wall, and he began to shiver uncontrollably.

"Can I put my clothes back on? I don't need hypothermia on top of everything else."

Silence.

"Listen, if I stand here much longer like this I am going to die. I don't want to die." Ranger's teeth were chattering so hard he was afraid he was going to break his teeth.

Suddenly a head popped around the side of the tree. A young man who looked to be in his late teens stared at him with fear in his eyes. He looked Ranger up and down and then nodded.

Without waiting for clarification on what the nod meant, Ranger quickly gathered his clothes and put them back on. It took a few minutes for the chills to leave his body, and as he rubbed his torso back to normalcy, he looked at the kid.

"Where's your dad?" Ranger asked when he felt he had regained control over his body.

The boy looked down at the ground and Ranger saw tears forming.

"Dead," came the whispered reply.

"Mom?"

"Same."

"How?"

"Deputies."

Ranger bit his lip. He hadn't run into any deputies recently, but he knew how ruthless they could be. He felt his heart go out to the kid. "Take me to your house."

The boy started to raise his rifle, but Ranger pushed the muzzle back toward the ground. "Not necessary. I'm not going to hurt you. I want to help you."

A flicker of hope passed through the kid's eyes but was snatched away with another coughing fit.

"You know what you have?" Ranger asked, strapping his quiver back around his waist and seating the bow across his chest.

"What do you mean?" The boy looked confused.

"You're coughing a lot. I assume you have something. Pneumonia? Cold? Tuberculosis?"

The boy simply shook his head, looking to be on the verge of crying again.

Ranger stepped up to him, put a hand on his shoulder and said, "Lead the way. You need to be out of this weather."

Without another word, the boy strode off toward his home.

The place was a two-story farmhouse and as they approached Ranger registered the sound of a generator. The kid had power. That meant he might also have running water, and he didn't want to get his hopes up, but maybe even hot water.

They walked up the patio stairs and the kid walked straight inside, shedding layers as he crossed the threshold.

"Where's your kitchen?" Ranger asked.

The boy pointed toward the back of the house and Ranger walked past him. Either the boy had come to realize he wasn't a threat, or he was too tired and sick to want to fight.

Ranger walked into the kitchen and saw dishes piled up in the sink. There were maggots feeding on an old piece of steak that stuck out from underneath the refrigerator. He opened the fridge and found rotten vegetables and some expired meats and cheeses. Some of the cheese looked like they had grown a full coat of fur.

As he went to close the fridge door he stopped and listened. He heard the sounds of whispering. Very carefully he bent down and wrapped his fist around the hilt of the knife in his boot. A floorboard creaked near him and in one smooth motion Ranger unsheathed the knife and thrust it forward, stopping inches from the stomach of a young girl. The boy cried out behind her and fumbled for his gun. Ranger immediately dropped the knife and raised his hands in front of his face.

"No no no. I dropped the knife. Leave the gun. I heard someone sneaking up on me is all. Knife's on the floor," Ranger said rapidly.

Neither the boy nor Ranger moved. The boy's hand still rested on the stock of the rifle, but he was making no move to pick it up. In the meantime, the little girl took two steps forward, picked up the knife, and held it out for Ranger to take. Ranger's eyes flicked from the girl to the boy, and he slowly took the knife from the girl and sheathed it in his boot again. The task done, Ranger raised his hand once more.

After a few tense moments, the boy removed his hand from the rifle and put it on the young girl's shoulder. Ranger watched the two of them, noting the similarities in their facial features. The tension still permeated the room, so Ranger found a chair and sat down, unburdening himself of his weapons to try and put the siblings more at ease.

"How long have you two been—" Ranger began, before seeing a set of eyes peering at him from the dark hallway. He changed his question: "How many are you?"

The boy, who looked on the verge of tears again, held up his hand, all five fingers splayed. A tear finally found its way down the boy's cheek and his little sister turned around and hugged him tight.

Ranger felt a tug at his heart. He had been running solo for nearly five years. When the end began, he had been optimistic that someone, anyone would change the way the country was headed. Surely there must be a force great enough to stamp out the corruption and selfishness that had permeated the national landscape. But the greed of men was too great, and when the leader gave his Cabinet the power to deputize whomever they desired, everything quickly got out of hand.

Now, even the most optimistic, level-headed people were hanging their heads and crying out about the end of days. Ranger never thought he would live in a time where the country would be put under martial law, and under a fickle, narcissistic leader at that. If he decided he didn't like people with brown eyes, that's who the deputies would focus and remove from society. Personal vendettas were broadcast to the citizens, and rewards offered to carry out bounties on those individuals. Suddenly, it was against the law to disagree with anything the leader said. Social media, once privatized, was now government owned and there was no statute of limitations on threats made in posts.

By the time the citizens realized what was truly happening, especially those who voted him in, it was too late. Nothing could be done, except to lay low or, if you happened to upset the leader, hide. Rights were stripped away from some and given freely to others. Some who earned favor were handsomely rewarded. But even those folks could slip up and find themselves on the wrong side of his wrath. So, everyone kept a low profile and tried not to arouse any suspicion whenever a deputy was near. What caomplicated things is the deputies were not required to wear any identification. They carried an official laminated card in their wallet, but even if anyone asked they could refuse to show it. Cloak and dagger was their game, and they were getting damn good at it.

Ranger was a wanted man, because he had made a quip, half in jest, about the leader and his inability to coherently manage a petting zoo, let alone a country. Fortunately, one of his closest friends was a deputy, and in a crisis of conscience tipped off Ranger that his house was going to be raided. He wasn't sure what happened to that friend, because being labeled a traitor was an immediately punishable Capital Offense. Anyone with a gun and a deputy card could shoot the offender dead with no consequences. There was never an inquiry into whether the person truly committed the 'crime' they were accused of, because no one cared.

Being on the run wasn't as difficult as it might seem. The leader changed his mind and focus so often that many 'traitors' and 'war criminals' were forgotten. Out of sight, out of mind. There was still a database, and when Ranger ran across deputies holding a tablet, he knew a facial scan would mean his death in an instant. Thus far he had been able to avoid such scans, but he felt his luck would eventually run out.

Many had imagined the end would come in the form of a bomb or an incurable disease running rampant, but as the old saying goes, 'The world didn't end with a bang…"

Other nations essentially quarantined his country. No one in or out. Border patrols were increased to ensure the 'infection' didn't spread. One news report from another country warned: "We will treat anyone who attempts to cross into our country as an invasive species. There is a moral decay present in your country which must be cut off in order for the rest of the world to survive. We understand this means many great citizens of your country are trapped in the madness, but isolation is the only option if we hope to regain the proper balance on this planet. May God have mercy on the souls of those who were in the wrong place at the wrong time, and may God's vengeance strike down those who willingly perpetrated the heinous atrocities the rest of the world has had to witness."

"There were six of us until a couple weeks ago." The boy's voice overrode the trance Ranger was under, and he re-focused on the child. Hunger had again begun to cloud his thoughts.

"I'm sorry. When did your parents pass?" Ranger looked around and noticed that all five children were huddled together on the opposite side of the kitchen.

The boy cleared his throat and said, "Almost a year ago." A look of confusion furrowed his brow. "I…think. It's been hard to keep track of the time properly."

Ranger nodded his head. "What's your name?"

"Gray," came the quick response.

"How old are you, Gray?"

"Sixteen next month." Another hesitation. "I'm pretty sure."

Ranger's stomach turned over, causing him to hunch forward in his seat for a minute. When he had gotten his breathing under control, he looked up at Gray. "Do you have anything edible in here?"

Gray thought for a moment and then responded, "Half a loaf of bread and some beef jerky."

"And a fruit roller," the little girl piped in, before shrinking behind her big brother again.

A large sigh from Gray.

"Don't worry, I won't eat your fruit roller. But I would love to have some of the bread and jerky."

Gray opened his mouth to protest, but Ranger held up his hand to silence him. "I am on your land, because I have been hunting a buck for the last few days. He has eluded me thus far, but I think I was fairly close to finding him before you took your shot at me."

The boy's eyes found the floor and his cheeks reddened.

Ranger leaned forward and said, "You did the right thing. You are protecting your family. You don't know me from Adam."

Gray's eyes flicked up then back to the floor.

"I mentioned the buck," Ranger continued, "because if I can find him I can dress him and portion out meat for you, so you have something to feed your siblings."

The little girl started to giggle, and Ranger raised his eyebrow. "Why would you dress a deer? Mama didn't have any dresses, but I could find some socks to put on him."

Despite the desperation Ranger was feeling, he let out a low laugh. "Dressing means cutting open the deer and utilizing every part of it. The skin can be made into clothing, the meat is good for eating, the antlers can be sharpened into weapons."

As he spoke, Ranger watched the little girl's face grow pale and tears begin to slide down her cheeks. He looked to Gray, but Gray seemed to understand the importance of the conversation.

"Lace, you know that meat comes from animals. That's all he's talking about. And we need to live. Let's listen to him. I think he wants to help us."

Ranger nodded his head and tried to smile, but it felt fake. "If you'll let me sleep in a bed and take a shower I will find that buck tomorrow and teach you," he pointed at Gray, "how to field dress it so you can continue to hunt animals and keep surviving."

Gray nodded. "You can sleep in mom and dad's room."

A gasp from his siblings, who had mostly stayed silent, echoed through the room.

Gray turned to them and said, "I know. It's not ideal, but he says he wants to help and if we don't let him we will starve. We've hardly eaten anything in the last week or so. I want to eat. I need to eat."

Slowly, one by one, the kids nodded their heads.

"Good," Gray said, and turned to the other boy in the group. "Michael, can you please go fetch the loaf of bread and jerky?"

The young girl chimed in with, "He can have a fruit roller too if he wants."

Ranger shook his head and replied, "I want you to save those for yourself. They sound very important."

Michael shuffled out of the room and re-entered moments later with a slightly moldy hunk of bread and a baggie of beef jerky. Ranger took them with a muttered thank you and told himself he would only eat a little. Enough to give him a bit of energy. But when he popped the first bite of bread into his mouth his base instincts took over and the loaf was nearly gone by the time he stopped. The jerky disappeared before Ranger realized he was eating it. Only when he looked at the faces of the children did he comprehend what he had done. They all stared at him, horrified, as he ate the last of their food stores.

A lump formed in Ranger's throat, making it difficult to swallow the bread that was in his mouth. When he finally was able to force it down, he said, "I'm sorry." He didn't know what else to say.

Gray silently walked up to him and took the tiny chunk of bread out of Ranger's hand. He then handed a piece to each of his siblings, leaving himself with only crumbs. The children half-heartedly attempted to give Gray some of their bread, but Gray was having none of it.

Ranger leaned forward and noticed that the sun still had a ways to go before it retired for the evening, so he looked at Gray and said, "If you can show me where to take a shower I can get back out and find that buck."

———

There wasn't any hot water, but Ranger felt somewhat refreshed. The food had done wonders for his energy, and he dressed to go out and find the buck. He inspected his legs, running a finger along the extensive scarring. Five years on the run had not been easy, but he felt like he was finally getting closer to his goal. He still hadn't worked out the details of what he would do when he reached his destination; there were hundreds of miles to travel.

After he dressed, Ranger walked down the stairs to the front door. The children were all sitting on the bench in the main hallway and when Gray saw him he jumped to his feet, rifle in hand. "I'm coming with you."

Ranger shook his head, gathered his bow and arrow and knife and opened the front door. "Take care of your siblings. I'll be back as soon as I'm able."

He was about to step through the when it slammed in front of him. A slow burn of anger crept into his chest, and he looked at Gray, who was glaring defiantly at him.

"You say you want to teach me how to do all this so I can take care of my family. How am I supposed to learn if you don't show me everything?" The boy's breath came in hot rasps through his nostrils. Clearly he was upset.

Ranger stared at Gray for a long time. Gray never once wavered in his glare back at him.

Finally, Ranger nodded his head and said, "You're right. You need to come with me. But you need to do everything I say. Understand?"

Gray blinked twice, quickly, his anger abating rapidly. "Thank you," was all he could manage, the fight gone out of him. He tightened his grip on the rifle, but Ranger shook his head.

"The less noise we make the better. Leave the gun."

Outside, Ranger knelt down, his knees crackling as he did. He took a large chunk of snow and started rubbing it all over his clothing. Gray tilted his head to the side, trying to figure out what exactly Ranger was doing.

Ranger noticed the boy staring and said, "I'm trying to get rid of odors that might alert the buck. The last thing we need is for him to catch our scent and get spooked. This isn't a perfect system, but it'll have to do for now."

Gray took a handful of snow and ran it over his clothing the best he could.

They finished and moved to the edge of the forest. There Ranger dug through the snow and found the actual ground. He grabbed a chunk of dirt and grass and began rubbing it over his skin and clothes.

"The more we smell of earth, the less alarming we will be to our prey," Ranger explained. Gray took up the task and soon both of them were as close to unalarming as Ranger figured they could be in the present circumstances.

Gray took a step toward the woods, but Ranger stayed him with a hand. "First we need to check for tracks. Hoof prints are ideal, but scat will be informative as well."

"Yeah, scat," Gray replied, nodding his head a little too vigorously.

Ranger couldn't help but smile. "Scat is a polite term for deer shit."

Color rose to Gray's cheeks. "Oh," was all he could manage.

Ranger tapped Gray's shoulder with the back of his hand and pointed into the forest. "See the tracks? Rabbit or possibly fox."

Gray scanned the ground and when he thought he saw something he pointed. "Is that something?" he asked tentatively.

It took a moment for Ranger to find what Gray was pointing at, but when he did he clapped the boy on his shoulder. "That is a great something! Broken branches are usually indicative of a larger animal. Could be our buck. Let's move. But we need to move slowly and methodically. We are hunters now."

Gray nodded.

A few minutes later they came across a clearing and Gray decided to ask the question that had apparently been plaguing him during the journey. "What's your name?"

"Ranger."

"Is that your real name?" Gray asked quietly.

"Is Gray yours?"

The boy looked away, abashed.

"Your parents taught you well. Real names can be dangerous these days."

The praise perked the boy up again. Ranger felt for him. He was a teenager whose parents were murdered, and he had been forced to grow up quickly; take on the care of five siblings, now four, and provide everything for them, not knowing if someone with ill intent would show up on the doorstep one day. They were isolated and probably unaware of the extent of the damage in the country, only relying on what information their parents had given them before dying.

Internet access was limited to specific public locations and was highly restricted. Only information beneficial to the leader and his cronies was allowed. Hackers tried on occasion to break through the firewalls and encryptions, but so far none had succeeded in turning the tide back toward a free flow of ideas. The last article Ranger read online boasted about how the latest round of hackers had been found and decapitated for their crimes. There were pictures. Their hands were missing too, because the deputies said those were the weapons they used to commit their treason. The problem was that deep fakes and altered images using AI and other programs could easily have altered the images. Hopefully, the hackers were still in hiding, but the leader wouldn't want that to be public knowledge. Better to communicate their executions as a deterrent to any others attempting to do the same.

There was a rustling at the edge of the clearing and Ranger moved only his eyes to get a glimpse of what it was. A snow-white rabbit sat chewing on a twig near a holly bush. Instinct took over and Ranger nocked an arrow and let it fly. His aim was true, and the rabbit fell on its side, its legs twitching.

Unfortunately, Ranger hadn't had time to warn Gray that dying rabbits screamed. He hadn't even known until the first rabbit he killed. Glancing over at Gray he saw the boy was crying and his hands were covering his ears. Ranger shook his head once and Gray slowly removed his hands from the sides of his face.

"If you're going to be doing this you have to face reality head on. If you falter, if you turn away, you lose your prize. Don't ever let that happen or you and your siblings will starve."

Gray slowly nodded his head. Ranger could tell the kid was trying to keep himself from dissociating, so he swiftly moved to the rabbit and slit its throat to make the screaming stop.

Gray bent over and retched. Ranger was not without sympathy for the boy. Nature was a cruel mistress, especially when there is no preparation for the necessary violence needed to live.

Ranger hung the rabbit by its haunches from the nearest tree to drain the blood, and while it did he cleaned his knife and checked on Gray.

"Eat some snow. Make sure it's clean. Eat some of the snow, wash out your mouth."

The boy did as he was told. And by the time Gray had scooped up his third handful of snow Ranger was ready to finish the job with the rabbit.

With the exception of brief instructions throughout the process, both Ranger and Gray remained completely silent while Ranger took the rabbit apart. The man could sense a shift within the boy. A little more armor was added to his psyche. Growing up too fast created nearly unbearable growing pains. Some he came across were unable to deal with those pains and had chosen a different path. He didn't want this young man to even consider that an option.

As if reading Ranger's mind, Gray stated, "As long as my siblings are alive I can't even entertain an thought of leaving them."

Ranger felt his heart sink in his chest. Gray had told him he wouldn't do anything drastic, but the caveat frightened him. "And if all your siblings were gone?"

A light breeze rustled through the clearing, stirring up eddies of snow. Gray stood silent for a long while before whispering his answer. "I don't know."

They stood silently for a few moments, before Ranger responded, "Well, let's get them all fed, shall we?" And he proceeded to show Gray the process of field dressing a rabbit.

═══════

Over the next week the children became more curious about the new adult that had moved in with them temporarily. Ranger and Gray had failed so far in finding the buck, but they did have some luck with various small creatures and birds, as well as two beavers Ranger trapped. He set to the task of showing Gray how to tan the hides of the critters. Later, they would make warm clothing out of them. Rabbit fur mittens, squirrel moccasins, and other items to help keep him and his siblings warm during the long winter.

Everyone perked up by the third day. They were getting a steady diet of protein. The children were all still too lean for Ranger's liking, but at least they were eating.

Ranger noticed that Gray ate the least at every meal, so he began saving a little of his own meat and handing it over to him during their nightly lessons. At first Gray refused the food, but when Ranger threatened to tell his siblings about what he was doing, he quickly relented.

On the third night, while Gray labored over the sewing technique on the rabbit hide from the first one they caught, Gray decided to open up to Ranger.

"You want to know why my parents were killed?" Gray asked, slightly distracted.

"If you want to tell me, I'll listen," Ranger replied.

"For three years after the leader came into power they offered our house as a safe haven. If you were any of the things that the leader despised, my parents had a place for you. There are so many secret hiding places, and not one of them is easy to find."

Gray lapsed into silence, but Ranger felt the right thing was to keep his own silence, so he stirred the vat holding a few different hides for tanning and stared off into the distance.

"You have walked by at least five hiding spots since you've been here and haven't noticed any of them," Gray finally continued.

Ranger thought about it and realized the kid was right. He hadn't even suspicioned that something might be off about the house.

Gray took a deep, shuddering breath. "If you had the wrong eye color on the wrong day, we would hide you until the leader forgot about that particular issue. If you liked the wrong person, we would welcome you in with open arms. I was in my early teens when this was all happening."

Gray hissed through his teeth and Ranger saw that he had stabbed his finger with the needle he was using. When Ranger moved to help the boy, Gray shook his head and kept talking.

"What my parents were doing seemed right. What the deputies were doing felt wrong. But it was all so confusing. Rumors started going around about us and deputies started showing up, but most of them were so hopped up on power that they weren't thorough. They could never find a single person or hideaway. But the stress was getting to my parents. They were so tense all the time."

The boy's voice caught in his throat, and he cleared it before he continued.

"I tried to lighten the mood. I tried to be the perfect son so there was one less thing they had to worry about. I took on more responsibility with my siblings. Nothing seemed to help. They continued to hide people and dodge the deputies. And everything seemed to be working out great. Except my mom and dad were going gray. And they weren't that old. I started having panic attacks, which frightened them, because what if I had a panic attack when a deputy was at the house, and I gave away our secret."

Gray had stopped sewing and was staring at the hide as if he were trying to burn a hole through it with his eyes.

"One day a new deputy came by. He used to be the basketball coach at my middle school. He knew our family. My dad always said he was one of the smartest people he knew, and it boggled his mind that he chose to coach basketball for seventh and eighth graders. I never fully understood anything my dad tried to explain after he had conversations with Coach Chance. But I was fascinated anyway.

"So, Coach started to come by, acting all friendly and talking to my mom and dad about how unfair it was what the leader was doing and how he had usurped his power and needed to be taken down a notch. We didn't know he was a deputy at first. And then he would tell me how much he missed coaching us all and that he wished my parents would let me come back to school."

Tears were making their way down the boy's cheeks, but Ranger kept his distance, trying not to breathe too loudly for fear of missing a word of the kid's story.

Gray's voice wavered as he continued. "After about two months of Coach visiting us, he started telling me about his thoughts on right and wrong and laws and everything having to do with what was happening here in the country. He told me it was our civic duty to abide by the law, even if they seemed unfair and maybe even a bit wrong. I was confused, because he had been ragging on the leader every time he came to our house.

"I asked him if he liked the leader, and he laughed and shook his head. I was relieved. 'But we all have a responsibility to do the right thing,' he told me. Then he told me about a house he had been to where the family was hiding some very bad people. I asked him what they had done that was so bad, but he shrugged it off and kept on with his story.

"'The point is,' he said, 'The family admitted to what they were doing and all they got was a little slap on the wrist. No harm no foul.' And then he kept saying things about moral obligations and being blameless in the eyes of the country. I didn't know what he wanted from me, but a pit in my stomach had begun to grow. I could feel a panic attack coming. I thought it must be because of who we were hiding. And he had said," Gray's voice cracked, but he spoke through the emotion, "He said the other family was just warned not to do it again."

Ranger saw the distress in Gray's face, the absolute anguish in his features, and goosebumps crawled over his skin.

"So I told Coach…" A sob wracked the boy's frame, and he couldn't speak for a long time. When he finally had control enough over his emotions to continue, he stared Ranger in the eye with a ferocity that frightened him a little.

Gray continued, his voice catching and small sobs escaping his throat. "I'm just a kid. I didn't know what I was doing. I thought I was helping."

Ranger stood up. He knew where this was going, but he desperately wanted to be wrong.

The emotion changed Gray's voice so Ranger had to strain to hear the rest.

"We were hiding a family and I told Coach where to find them." Another loud burst of crying, and then, "He looked like he had won a prize. His face changed. I begged him to do like what happened at the other house. I begged him to tell my parents not to do it again and for that to be the end of it."

The boy was weeping at this point, but he seemed determined to finish his story. Ranger waited.

Finally, the dam burst and through sobs, Gray said, "I killed my mama and papa. I killed them. It was all my fault."

And as Ranger rushed over to hold the boy, he heard the last crushing confession, "And I tried to keep my baby brother alive. I tried so hard. I tried so so hard. But I couldn't do it."

With his confession complete Gray collapsed, but Ranger was close enough to catch him before he could do any damage to himself. Ranger found that he was crying too. He held the boy and let him weep in his arms.

Eventually, the sobbing subsided into whimpers and fractured breaths and Ranger said, "The world is confusing. We are told from every side what is right and what is wrong, what we should believe and what we should condemn. But the problem is, one side says one thing is right while the other says it's horribly wrong. We're so lost in our own ideologies and prejudices that we forget beneath all the fighting we are all human beings. We forget that humanity is what really matters. You did what you thought was right. You were deceived. You were lied to. An adult you trusted manipulated you and you feel responsible.

"When I was growing up, if you were too trusting you were called gullible. We've been set up to be cynical from a young age. Hide everything and when you finally show even a portion of your true self you have to cross your fingers that they won't use it against you. A grown man took advantage of you, and you think that's your fault? No way. Never.

"Listen to me Gray, you did not kill your parents. You did not kill your baby brother. You did the best you could with the information you had, and it all went sideways. But none of that is your fault. Keep fighting. Fight for your siblings. Fight for what is right and good."

Ranger held the boy out at arm's length and smiled through his tears. "And most of all, keep fighting for yourself. Yeah?"

Gray sniffed a couple times, staring directly back at Ranger, and then he nodded. "I'll try," he whispered.

Ranger hugged the boy again. "That's all you can do."

They stood there for a long moment, and when Ranger finally opened his eyes he saw the buck standing at the edge of the forest watching them intently. Ranger turned slowly to one side so Gray could see it, and when he felt the boy's body tense Ranger knew he had a visual. "You want to go catch that buck?" he whispered.

Gray nodded his head slowly.

═══════

It had been nearly a week since Ranger left the kids in the capable hands of their eldest sibling. Gray had taken to the task of hunting, dressing, and tanning the animals very quickly, so he felt confident leaving them to continue his own task. The young girl had come up to him with an envelope in her hand when he was leaving and told him he couldn't open it until he was at least 150,000 feet away, because that would mean he was far enough away to get a letter. Inside he found a few little tokens of appreciation from each of the kids, a note written by the youngest, and two fruit rollers.

Although he trained Gray well, there still wasn't an excess of food when he left, so he hadn't taken any of their stores and had saved the fruit rollers for as long as he could. But he had difficulty finding actual food to eat, so he had been forced to eat them sooner than intended. They were very good.

The sun was descending over the horizon when he heard the sounds of sprinklers. And where there were sprinklers he imagined there would be vegetables or fruit. Cautiously, he made his way toward the sound and when he walked over the crest of a hill he saw paradise in front of him. Banks of vegetables and an orchard of fruit trees lay in front of him like a smorgasbord. His mouth immediately started salivating. Normally he wouldn't be one to take from what wasn't his, but the gnawing hunger in his stomach overrode his moral principles.

As he wandered between the rows, looking for anything edible, he realized that it was probably still too early in spring for anything to be ready. Row after row of plant sprouts met his eye and he was becoming discouraged when he heard the sound of a gun hammer being pulled back. Immediately his hands went up and his thoughts went to deputies. If this was a deputy with a tablet he would be done for.

"Turn around slowly," a gravelly voice told him.

Ranger did as he was told and was surprised to find an elderly gentleman standing five feet from him, his finger on the trigger of a .9mm.

"Who said you could steal my vegetables?" the man growled at Ranger.

"I'm sorry. I haven't really eaten in a couple weeks. I was just looking for something, anything to help with my hunger pangs." The stress of the situation and the lack of food in his stomach conspired to send Ranger's head spinning and he watched as the world rotated around him and after a few moments he met the earth with a soft thud.

———

Ranger slowly opened his eyes, stars dancing in the middle of his vision, and found himself staring at a ceiling. Confusion, followed by panic. He sat up too fast, watched as the world revolved around him, and laid back down with a groan.

"I wouldn't do that if I were you," a woman's voice said.

Slowly, he turned his head to the side and found an elderly woman with a kind smile staring at him from across the room.

"Frank told me he caught you trying to steal our vegetables. When he came back to the house he told me how you had passed out and I made him grab the wheelbarrow and go back to get you."

Off the look on Ranger's face she said, "He may be getting on in age, but he's still strong as a bull." There was a slight twinkle in her eye as she said it.

"Where am I?" Ranger managed.

"You are on Frank and Ethel's farm," Ethel said proudly.

She stood up from the chair where she had been seated and patted Ranger on the leg. "I bet you're real hungry. Why don't you join us for a late supper?"

Before Ranger could respond she was out the door and walking down the hall. "Bathroom is two doors down. We set out a towel and cleaned your clothes. Everything is in there waiting for you."

Ranger lifted the covers and discovered he was completely naked. He waited another minute or so until he was certain Ethel had moved away from the hall and then made a mad dash for the bathroom. Dizziness hit him, but he shook it off and made it before needing to steady himself on the sink.

True to her word, his clothes were neatly folded and sitting on a shelf and there was a towel and washcloth draped over a rod near the shower. He stepped into the shower and turned on the water, bracing himself for the cold. The spray hit him, and he sucked in a sharp breath through his teeth. There was a bar of soap and a bottle of shampoo, and he cleaned himself thoroughly. He even imagined the water was heating up, and then he noticed the steam. The water was getting hotter and soon it was almost too hot to handle, but he let the water scald his body and cleanse him.

When he finally got out of the shower he noticed a toothbrush and toothpaste sitting on the edge of the sink. He didn't remember them being there before he got in the shower, but he didn't particularly care. His teeth hadn't been brushed in a long time. Ranger mused that a dentist would be appalled. He used too much toothpaste, but by the time he was done his teeth were practically sparkling.

Refreshed and wearing clean clothing, he made his way down the hall and down the stairs into the dining area, where Frank and Ethel were sitting, waiting for him.

Frank smiled at him and said, "Sorry about the scare earlier, young man. Didn't mean to have you pass out on me."

Ranger shook his head and replied, "No worries. I shouldn't have been on your land in the first place."

The smell of the food hit him and he felt faint again, so he sat quickly at the table and saw they had already dished him out a heaping plate of meat, vegetables, fruits, and starches. He looked across at them both, their plates empty.

"Sorry," Ethel said. "We tried to wait, but we were quite hungry ourselves. It takes a lot of energy to haul a full-grown man up a flight of stairs at our age."

Ranger opened his mouth, clearly embarrassed, but Ethel waved off the feeling immediately.

"We wouldn't have done it if we thought you were a deputy." She paused, a sly look in her eyes. "Plus, we looked through all your stuff and didn't find a card."

"Dig in," Frank said.

The first bite Ranger took made him swoon. The meat was juicy, the vegetables seasoned perfectly, the fruit practically melted in his mouth, and the mashed potatoes were extra creamy with a healthy helping of garlic. He made it halfway through the plate before anyone spoke again.

"What's your name?" Ethel asked.

"Ranger," he replied through a mouthful of carrots.

"Funny name," she said, and when he looked up at her he knew she was aware it was fake.

"I'm wanted. Can't be too careful." He smiled at her shyly.

"Do something awful, did you?" Frank piped in. "Like saying a bad word or crossing the street at the wrong time of day on a Tuesday?"

Ranger chuckled. "Something like that."

"So, Ranger, you just aimlessly running across the country until you find someplace safe to hunker down?" Ethel asked.

Ranger was beginning to think Frank and Ethel weren't as out of touch as he first assumed. Their questions and thoughts were very pointed.

He decided to avert the questioning for a moment with one of his own. "What did you two do before," and he gestured to the air with his fork, "all of this?"

"Well," Ethel began, grabbing a cookie and dunking it in her tea, "We have lived here for most of our married life. I've taken care of the farm since the beginning. But Frank, he was an agent. One of the best."

"Agent? Like a spy?" Ranger asked while scooping another bite of food into his mouth.

"Yeah, I worked for an intelligence agency. Black Ops shit," Frank said with a smile.

Ethel slapped him on the shoulder. "Watch your language, old man. It's not very becoming."

Frank rolled his eyes and laughed. "She made me into one of the best." He held up his hand when Ethel opened her mouth to interject. "No, no. I'm serious, Ethel. Son, I would come home knowing full well that if they ever knew I told my wife about everything I was doing I would be fired…or worse. But what they didn't know wouldn't kill them. Ethel and I share everything, always have. So, I would come home and tell her what I was working on, and she would ask questions that hadn't crossed my mind to ever think about asking. It allowed me to think outside of the confines of the job and be more creative with my techniques. She wasn't in the thick of it, so she had a completely different perspective. It was, and still is, the best partnership I've ever been a part of."

Ranger envied them. They had each other and he knew they would back each other until the day they died. He had no one.

They all let the silence fill the room, Ranger with a fork full of food suspended halfway to his mouth, Frank and Ethel watching him intently with the slightest hint of a smile on both their faces.

Finally, Frank cleared his throat, snapping them all out of the moment.

Ethel sat back in her chair and said, "Ranger, I want you to tell me what your intention is with traveling across the country. No bullshit."

Frank opened his mouth in mock outrage at her use of the curse word, which made them both laugh.

Ranger took his time chewing a bite of food, unsure how much he wanted to tell them. In his gut he felt that he could trust them, but flashes of his conversation with Gray wormed their way into his consciousness.

He decided he needed Frank to answer one question for him before he felt safe enough to tell them the truth. "Why did you leave the agency, Frank?"

"When you're supposed to be a professional, protecting the world from actual threats and dangers, and someone comes along and tells you to follow up on leads that personally affect them, you start to question your position in that profession." Frank shrugged his shoulders.

"He wasn't anybody's personal errand boy, but he also knew how dangerous it would be to flip him the bird and try to ride off into the sunset. So, he silently stopped going to work and by the grace of God no one has come looking for him," Ethel added.

Ranger thought a moment longer and then nodded. "Well, if you're going to kill me I guess this is it. But I think I can trust you."

"Up to you," Ethel responded.

"I am on my way to kill the leader," Ranger said.

As the words left his mouth he felt as though he couldn't breathe. He hadn't told a living soul what his pilgrimage was about, and now two people knew. And he waited for the bullet he knew was coming. Instead, he saw the couple exchange knowing glances and Ethel stood up from the table and started to remove the dishes.

"Do you know who Dietrich Bonhoeffer is, Ranger?" Ethel asked, still clearing the table.

"The name rings a bell," Ranger replied.

"Bonhoeffer was a German Lutheran pastor who saw the evils of the Nazis and denounced them and what they stood for. He went so far as to assist in a plot to assassinate Hitler. He was marched to the gallows at Flossenbürg Concentration Camp for his part in that plot," Frank said.

"But he understood the gravity of what they were attempting to do. The moral gray of taking a life to save countless other lives. I'm sure you've done the mental gymnastics and have wrestled with yourself over this idea of yours, but you have to be all in if you want to succeed," Ethel added.

"So, you two think this is the right thing to do?" Ranger asked, hoping the answer would be simple.

"Sometimes it's not about right and wrong, but about necessity. If we allow an evil to continue to tear apart the fabric of humanity, what does that say about us as human beings? Is it possible to simply dethrone this person and allow people to return to a sense of normalcy? Or is it too far down the line?" Ethel suddenly sounded very tired.

"What Ethel is trying to say is, if you look at the followers of this man, are they so fervently under his control that they would make things better upon hearing their leader has been killed? Or will it incite them to a fever pitch that will make everything worse?" Frank shrugged his shoulders, as if to say he didn't have the answer either.

Ranger thought a moment before speaking. "This is why it has taken me years to start my journey. I thought maybe it would be like a bad dream that would slowly fade from the minds of everyone involved, but it's only gotten worse. I don't know what the solution is, but if we continue to do nothing…" Ranger left the thought unfinished.

A deep silence descended over the kitchen, the only sounds were Ethel continuing to clear the table. Ranger tensed his body, feeling the urge to help with the dishes, but Ethel put a stop to it immediately. "Nuh uh. If you get up from that table I will break your arm so you physically can't help."

Frank smiled at his wife and then turned to Ranger. "We are living in a time that none of us wanted to live in. Call me an eternal optimist or call me dense, but I believe there is always hope, no matter how slim. There will always be people out there who understand the humanity of the situation. Right now, it feels as though that section of people is outnumbered, but it also makes me think that the loudest people aren't always the ones on the right side of history. Look for the quiet ones, the people who silently work toward peace and understanding. They have strong voices but are discerning when to use them to actually be effective. Those are the ones that will turn the tide."

Ethel put a hand on Frank's shoulder. "What you have set out to do may be the only course of action left. But it's possible that there are other avenues yet to pursue. The leader has taken away our access to the world, cutting off communications with other countries, limiting our internet to fit his propaganda. Is it possible that there are other people with the same thought as you? Is it possible that there are hundreds of people working on how to resolve this crisis? Maybe even thousands of people? Revolution takes time, making a change takes time."

Ranger listened to Frank and Ethel and the wheels turned in his head. They weren't sowing doubts into him, but they *were* making sense.

He offered, "I don't know the right answer, either. Maybe there isn't a single right answer. Maybe it's an amalgamation of concepts that when put together provides an outcome that's a best-case scenario for humanity. All I know is that I can no longer sit by and watch the country I love disappear into a chasm of hatred. It's possible that as I journey other ideas will come to me, but right now I only hold the one in my head." Ranger was grateful to these people. More grateful than he could ever express.

Frank suddenly smiled at Ranger. "You seem like an intelligent young man who is desperate for a breath of fresh air. We'll get there, one way or another. Faith goes a long way in times like these."

Ethel grabbed Ranger's hand and said, "It's late. Stay the night and then we will say our goodbyes in the morning after you've filled your belly one more time."

Ranger nodded his head in agreement and retired to the room he had woken up in hours earlier. He anticipated nightmares, but before he knew it the sun was peeking through the window and the smell of breakfast enticed him to wake.

———

The three of them stood on the front porch, surveying the crops in the mid-morning light. Ranger held out a piece of paper to Ethel.

"There is a family of children I came across whose parents were killed by deputies. I don't know if there is any way for you to get to them, or if you would even want to bring them here, but they could definitely use some help. The oldest is a great hunter and he knows how to tan hides. There is a deep sadness in him. I wrote down the address and a phrase you need to say to Gray, the oldest, if you decide to try and contact them."

Ethel furrowed her brow. "Phrase?"

Ranger smiled. "It's my way of vouching for you. It's so they know you're safe."

Ethel smiled back. "We'll do what we can. No promises. Maybe you should have stayed with them."

A long silence grew between them and then Ranger said, "Maybe."

Ethel hugged him for a long time and when she pulled away she said,

"I hope you discover your best plan while you travel. Frank and I believe in your mission."

Frank stepped up to Ranger, holding out a set of keys. "We have an old truck. She's not much, but she's got wheels and gasoline."

Ranger shook his head. "I really appreciate the offer, but the random checkpoints throughout the country concern me. The more invisible I can stay, the further I believe I can make it without incident."

Frank nodded his head and said, "Thought you might say that. I put your backpack over there by that old Oak. I bid you farewell and good luck, young man. Remember to find humanity before committing to an ideology."

Ranger nodded, afraid if he spoke he would start to cry. He noticed that Ethel was crying for the both of them. When he started his journey Ranger never thought anything could interfere with his end goal. But now he had questions, and he was fairly certain the questions needed to be engaged in order for him to keep his soul. He might still need to go through with his ultimate plan, but now his mind was open to alternatives, should they present themselves.

As he walked down their long driveway he noticed that his sack felt heavier than it did when he arrived. He waited until he was out of sight of the farmhouse to peek inside, and he found meats, vegetables, fruits, cheese, and two canteens filled with water. There was also a note:

Thank you for visiting us. Along with the food you will find some random baubles that might be useful if you find yourself in the position of needing to trade with someone. If you make it out of this alive, please come back and let us know how it all went. — Frank and Ethel

———

It was early June when Ranger ran into his first major problem. He was keeping to forest paths as much as possible, but had come across a seemingly impassable chasm. Looking to the left and to the right he needed to make a decision. He knew if he went left it would eventually dump him out on the road, if the chasm continued that far. If he went right he didn't know how far he would have to walk to find a place to safely pass. It could be one mile or it could be a hundred.

He decided to test his luck going left and when he finally saw the gap in the earth floor begin to taper he realized he could also see a main road through the trees. Slowing his pace and grabbing hold of his bow, he inched along the edge of the precipice until the jump across was manageable. Holding his breath, he took ten steps back and as he ran he thought he heard someone scream. This brought him to a halt before the gap and he turned his ear toward where he had heard the sound.

A moment later he heard two people laughing, followed by an angry exclamation and the sound of metal smacking flesh. Ranger closed his eyes, knowing that interfering could jeopardize his mission. He tried to imagine what Frank and Ethel would do and remembered that the whole purpose of his journey was to help people to feel safe once again in a country they once relied on for protection.

Ranger snuck toward the sound and when there were only a few trees separating him and the road he saw two men with semi-automatics standing near a man and a woman. The man was on the ground, blood pouring from his nose, and the woman had her back to a tree, arms at her sides. Realization hit Ranger that these two had run across two deputies, and those deputies were abusing their power to do whatever they wanted with these two.

The deputy closest to the woman took out a knife and cut the straps off the dress she was wearing, causing it to fall, exposing her bra underneath. Ranger saw the man on the ground contort his face and tense as if he were about to rise and fight. The deputy standing over him leaned down and put the muzzle of his gun to the top of his head.

"You try anything, pretty boy, and I squeeze the fucking trigger." He pressed the gun harder against the man's head and laughed.

From the ground, the man with the bloody nose looked up and made eye contact with Ranger, which caused Ranger's heart to beat faster. If the man alerted the deputies to his presence it would be over for him. But the man retained his composure and simply mouthed the word, *please* and then looked back down at the ground and spat out a wad of phlegm infused with blood.

At the tree, the other deputy had placed his left hand above the woman's head and his right hand was moving lightly over her breastbone. All of his attention was on her bosom, and the lecherous look in his eyes made Ranger want to dry heave.

The arrow struck the man's hand, pinning him to the tree before he knew what was happening. It took him another few seconds to register the arrow sticking through his hand embedded in the tree, then his eyes widened, and he began to scream.

His fellow deputy turned toward the trees and sprayed bullets into the woods in an attempt to catch the perpetrator with a lucky shot. But Ranger had immediately moved and hidden below a slight rise in the earth.

When the initial gunfire stopped he peeked his head just enough to be able to see the road. The woman had moved away from the deputy who was pinned to the tree, and looked like he was about to pass out, and over to the man on the ground. Back together Ranger could tell they weren't sure exactly what to do. Ranger was so focused on them that he almost ducked too late as another barrage of bullets pounded into the trees and ground near him. Then a click and the sound of the deputy yelling in rage, "THESE GOD DAMN GUNS!!"

The arrow struck the deputy in his right calf and in his surprise he dropped his gun, which skittered across the pavement out of his reach. He tried to limp his way over to his weapon, but stopped when he saw Ranger emerge from the trees, another arrow nocked, bowstring taut.

"You try anything, pretty boy, and I let go," Ranger threatened.

The deputy dropped to the ground and started to whimper. Ranger looked to the other deputy and saw he was slumped against the tree, the only thing holding him up the arrow piercing his hand. A slow trail of blood was dribbling down the trunk.

Ranger saw the deputy on the road had an ankle holster and he yelled, "Take that other gun and toss it!"

For whatever reason, the deputy decided to play dumb. "I don't have another gun," he cried, his hand instinctively reaching toward his foot.

The second arrow zipped through the air, pinning the deputy's hand to his thigh. The man let out a scream and then promptly passed out. Ranger replaced his bow across his chest and grabbed the gun on the pavement and then the one in the deputy's ankle holster. He repeated the process with the other deputy and then placed the guns down in front of the man and woman.

For a second they cowered away from Ranger, but when he stepped away from the guns the man repeated his thanks over and over half legibly through the shattered mess of his face. The woman was regaining her composure and Ranger saw a fury light in her eyes. She simply nodded at Ranger and Ranger knew it was time to move on. He wasted no time disappearing back into the forest.

He was nearly a quarter mile away from the incident when he heard the steady staccato of gunfire followed by a primal scream of rage.

———

Ranger checked his map and realized how far he had actually walked. The fall leaves were slowly tumbling to the ground. He took a moment to take a sip from his canteen and then he continued his journey. He anticipated that he would reach his destination within the next few days.

The sounds of gunfire had become more frequent the closer he got to the end of the road. Of course, whenever he heard the sounds he would veer away from them until he could hardly hear anything outside of the ambience of nature. He felt like he was spiraling toward the epicenter, and a quiet discomfort began to settle in his stomach. There was a mixture of fear and accomplishment tugging at him from all sides.

Night was falling, the shadows in the forest becoming longer and more sinister. As the last light left the sky, Ranger dropped his satchel and opened it to eat the last of the vegetables he had pilfered a few days prior.

A gun to the back of his head made him freeze.

"I just want to eat a carrot. Is that okay?" he asked, trying to make the encounter not seem so desperate.

"Who are you and where did you come from?" A woman's voice. The gun did not waver.

"I have traveled all the way across the country. I am not a deputy. I will empty my pockets and step away and you can rifle through all my belongings. I won't try to stop you," Ranger responded.

He felt a slight increase in pressure from the gun and he took it as acceptance of his terms. Quickly, he emptied his pockets, the last bauble from Frank and Ethel tumbling to the ground, and then he turned them out showing there was nothing left.

Another push from the barrel. "Weapons too."

Ranger nodded once and did as he was told and then he stood up and walked twenty feet away, not looking back until he was told to stop.

When he did turn around he found himself looking at a young woman wearing rags who was filthy from head to toe. She held the gun on him for a moment longer and then her eyes flicked over his stuff. Still trying to aim the gun at Ranger, she opened his satchel and ran her fingers over the contents. Then she dumped the bag out and grabbed a couple carrots, shoving them in her pocket.

Ranger heard a rustling and looked past the woman to see a man who looked to be in his sixties step into the small clearing.

"What is going on here, Daisy?" he asked. Daisy tossed him an apple over her shoulder, which he caught deftly.

Ranger thought maybe the man would put a stop to the search, but he sat down on a fallen log and bit into the apple, the juice running down his chin into his beard.

"That is a good apple, stranger," the man said, clear appreciation in his eyes. "It's been a dog's age since I had an apple."

All Ranger could think to do was nod.

"What brings you into our woods?" the man asked, bits of apple flying out of his mouth.

"I have my reasons," Ranger replied tersely.

"Well, lah-dee-dah," the man said, chuckling.

He kicked a small stick at the woman he had called Daisy and asked, "You have a reason to be here?"

"Nah," she replied, shaking her head.

"Well okay then," the man said, leaning back, trying to get comfortable.

A long silence ensued while Daisy picked out whatever bits and bobs she wanted from Ranger's store of goods. Ranger lowered himself to the ground and sat with his legs crossed. He figured they weren't deputies, because they would have most likely killed him by now, or worse.

"What's it like over here?" Ranger asked.

The man shrugged. "Daisy, you got an opinion to share?"

"Nah," Daisy said again, shaking her head.

"Woman of few words, but many talents," the man said, pride shining through in his eyes.

Ranger let the silence settle back over the clearing and he even closed his eyes for a few minutes, utterly exhausted.

Finally, he felt a tap on his foot and looked up to see the man standing over him holding out a hand. "We don't really have anything, but we are more than happy to share what you have provided from your knapsack there."

Ranger took the hand and was pulled to standing. "Gee, how generous," he retorted sardonically.

"I know, right?" the man laughed and clapped Ranger on the back. The force of the man's hand made Ranger take a step forward, so he simply continued to walk.

They followed Daisy back to a small encampment. There were a few other people sitting around a small fire, including a couple children. The children waved as they entered camp and Daisy waved back, tossing them both an apple. They tore into them with ravenous pleasure.

The man grabbed Ranger's shoulder and directed him to one of the logs and pushed him down. Ranger felt the power the man possessed and had no intention of testing his mettle.

Both children sidled up next to Ranger and began asking questions at the same time. "Who are you? Where did you come from? Are you gonna stay with us? Got any more apples?"

Ranger couldn't help but smile and raised his hands to bring them to a grinding halt. "My name is Ranger, I come from across the country, I made acquaintances with Daisy and big man over there not too long ago, and I'm pretty sure you ate the last two apples."

The children expressed their displeasure at the last answer and sauntered back over to their previous seats.

"So, Ranger," the man said, rolling the name around his tongue as if tasting it for poison. "Tell me why you have traveled across this great country of ours."

Ranger had the feeling that if he refused the man's request he would find himself in a difficult spot very soon. So, he sighed and said, "I am trying to get the leader to stop this mass genocide."

Everyone looked up at him at that. Even Daisy, who had been gnawing at a carrot, stopped chewing and stared at him. The man nodded his head slowly.

"I'm Big Bob, and you already met Daisy. The rest of the names aren't important."

One of the kids let out a 'heeeeeyyy' but was silenced by one of the other adults.

"If Ranger here isn't willing to tell us his name, I don't feel obligated to give ours away." Big Bob looked around the circle and was met with no opposition.

"That's fair," Ranger stated.

Big Bob turned back to him and asked, "So, how do you plan on stopping the leader exactly?"

Ranger shrugged. "I'm not really sure. Without communications I had to make it this far so I could see what I'm up against. What are you all doing out here?"

"Surviving," Daisy said softly.

"Have you tried to do anything about what's happening?" Ranger asked, realizing these people might be able to give him a little insight into the inner workings of the leader and his deputies.

Big Bob pointed at Daisy and said, "You heard her answer."

Ranger simply nodded.

The children were yawning and Ranger watched as two of the adults picked them up and took them into one of the tents scattered around the perimeter of the clearing. When he turned to look around at the rest of the rag tag group he saw that Daisy was standing in front of him holding out his satchel. He took it, noting how much lighter it suddenly was, and thanked her.

"Your weapons are over there," she said, pointing to a tree that was away from the tents. Ranger took the hint and stood up.

He seated his bow across his chest again and replaced his knife in its sheath and stepped into the forest. Not even ten steps into his walk he heard the sound of someone sniffing. Before he had time to react, Big Bob stepped out from behind a tree in front of him.

"Ranger, I need to make one thing very clear before you continue your crusade," he said in a low voice.

Ranger nodded.

"If any of the deputies find us because of you, the leader will be the least of your concerns. Do you understand me?" The threatening undertone sent a single shiver through Ranger's body. In the right circumstances he would be a very dangerous man.

"I would expect nothing less," Ranger replied with as much courage as he could muster.

Big Bob assessed Ranger for a long moment and then nodded his head. "If you make it to the end of the road, try and find Raven. She might be able to help you." His eyes glazed over for a moment, nostalgia and things lost hitting him all at once. "If you and whoever else is trying to end this succeed, we will be forever in your debt."

Ranger stared at Big Bob and said, "The whole point of this is to destroy any debt. If we can go back to a world of kindness and understanding, no one owes anyone a thing. I hope you and your family get the chance to thrive. And I will do my part in trying to make that possible."

With that said, Ranger continued to walk, but Big Bob's voice rang out once more. "I would come with you, but…" He didn't finish the sentence, but Ranger could sense the regret and sadness in his voice.

Without looking back Ranger said, "Taking care of your own is what is important right now. I hope to see you again, Big Bob." And with that he slid deeper into the woods.

———

Three nights later Ranger found himself skirting the perimeter of deputies that surrounded the central building. There didn't appear to be any point of ingress, but Ranger wasn't as concerned about that quite yet. He wanted to study the deputies, their routines, their bathroom breaks, their changing of the guard. He had no doubt that the perimeter was watched around the clock. If he wanted any hope of an incursion, he would either have to wait for a mistake made by the deputies or find other people of the same ilk who were seeking the same prize.

Ranger still wasn't sure what he planned to do once he reached the leader, but he knew that if he wanted to stand a chance he needed a pretty large lucky break. So, he sat, and he watched, hour after hour, long enough for the sun to reappear on the horizon. Thus far he had found no chink in the armor. Every deputy was heavily armed. Most of them wore bulletproof vests. Not one of them seemed to doze off during their shift or even get distracted. Two deputies to a post, both looking opposite directions to cover the arc where someone could possibly attempt to sneak past. A deputy came out every two hours on the hour and made his way down the line, handing out coffees and then standing in place of anyone who needed to use the bathroom. Then the deputy would disappear back inside the central building to do who knew what until he reappeared once again. Each team took eight-hour shifts, and the rotation of fresh deputies meant that only one set moved away from the perimeter at a time. They had worked themselves into a finely tuned machine, and a seed of doubt nestled into Ranger's heart.

Not to be deterred, Ranger continued to work his way around the perimeter for the next few days until one night he passed by a tree and saw someone sitting on a downed log in front of the path. She was a lean woman who looked like she had been training for this eventuality within the country. Her hair was black and only her eyes were visible in the middle of the balaclava she wore.

"Raven?" Ranger took a stab.

If his question surprised her, she didn't show it. She just nodded her head.

"Big Bob told me I should find you," Ranger said matter-of-factly. He felt like the time for cageyness and paranoia was past. He wanted to end this, one way or another.

Raven stood up and walked toward Ranger. "Big Bob is a good man. Taught me everything I know."

It was Ranger's turn to nod. "He seems like someone you don't want to cross. Can we talk?"

"Pretty sure that's what we're doing," came the cheeky reply.

"Fair point," Ranger conceded. Then he continued, "I'm here to remove the leader from his position of authority. But it would appear that won't happen without the help of others."

"Astute," was all Raven said.

"The deputies surrounding the central building seem to be flawless. I can't figure a way past them."

A twinkle came to Raven's eyes, and she smiled as she said, "Tell me your observations."

Ranger told her all he had noticed, and her smile broadened, causing Ranger to believe she had a lynchpin that would make all his intel seem like child's play. He wasn't wrong.

"You seem to have a decent handle on the situation," Raven began. "However, you are missing the biggest piece of the puzzle." Ranger cocked his head to the side, but Raven held up a hand. "I'm not going to make you guess. Did you notice the tablets that every single one of the deputies carries with them?"

Ranger nodded.

"And did you happen to notice how often they look at those tablets?" Ranger's mouth dropped open, imagining where she was heading with this information. "Of course you didn't, or you would have mentioned it. Don't feel bad. We've been staking out the place for a few weeks now and only in the last few days did we realize we had the answer in front of us the whole time. I know, sounds so cliché when I say it out loud."

"They are being fed a constant stream of information on their tablets. Without them they are blind. They operate by rote. If you could somehow disrupt…" Ranger looked up to see Raven's broad smile. She was nodding her head.

"And we have a small team working on trying to hack into the tablets to give us an opening."

"How close are they?"

"I am not technical when it comes to electronics or technology, but they assure me we are no more than a few days out from gaining control over their devices." She paused and took a deep breath. "We also have a team devising a plan on what to do once we have access to their tablets."

Ranger bit the inside of his lip. "Could you issue directives that they would follow? Like, say, telling them to abandon their posts because the leader is in danger within the building. Get them to believe there has been a direct attack from underneath?"

"We may have to be a bit more subtle than that, but essentially we need to get rid of the deputy guards and find a way to the leader while minimizing casualties." Raven let her cool demeanor slip for a second, revealing a rage hidden just below the surface. But as fast as that rage showed itself it was hidden away as quickly.

"How can I help?" Ranger asked.

Raven thought for a long moment and then said, "I've got some ideas. Follow me."

***

Over the next few days Ranger integrated himself into the operation. He was tasked with helping craft a directive for the deputies once the hackers were able to infiltrate their tablets. The most surprising piece was finding out that they had acquired quite a few tablets, but much to his disappointment he learned that once a deputy disappeared or was found dead, their tablet was immediately decommissioned. A dormant virus sat inside the coding of each tablet rendering it useless as soon as they sent the activation code.

The team had managed to keep three of the tablets operational by eradicating the poisonous code before it could be activated, but the systems were still wiped clean. Having uninfected tablets provided them with the slim chance that they would be able to hack the system, thus setting their plans in motion.

The first snow fell the night they heard quiet applause from the IT tent. They all knew how important silence was, even though they were technically out of the earshot of the central building. Ranger and Raven rushed into the tent and saw the team smiling and hugging each other. They had done it. One of the tablets had a direct link to the ones carried by the deputies.

"So, we're in. We did it," Raven said, ecstatic.

One of the IT guys bobbled his head on his shoulders, "Well, yes and no. We are in, but we still need to somehow gain the clearance level to send messages without the upper echelon becoming suspicious." He held one finger in the air in triumph. "However, we now have access to see every message sent and all the schedules they have posted."

Raven hugged the man, whose shocked expression told Ranger it was the last thing he ever expected to happen. Ranger simply smiled.

When the hug had run its course, Raven asked the IT guy to show her the information that was coming through, which he gladly did. Ranger could still see the band of scarlet around the man's neck from the unexpected hug.

Raven held the tablet and watched as messages came through almost as fast as she could read. Ranger peered over her shoulder.

- Team A-5 Cooper and Carlson Rotate out T-13 minutes. Team B-7 Hoskins and Kramer will report.
- Disturbance near SE perimeter. Confirmed to be a rabbit. Unconcerned.
- Message from the leader: *Keep up the good work. You are doing the most important work of your life. I have never felt safer, which is all thanks to you.*

The messages continued to flow across the screen and Raven moved her finger to tap, but the IT guy grabbed it quickly, and he blushed with embarrassment. "We don't really know what they can see or not in terms of reciprocal communication, so we need to do a little more studying before attempting to dive into the entire system. It would really suck to get this far and then be found out before anything can be done."

Raven pulled her finger away from the screen and the IT guy realized he was still holding it and quickly let go. His whole face was a deep shade of red now.

Raven surprised the man again by leaning in close and whispering something in his ear. His mouth dropped open, and he unsuccessfully tried to suppress a grin. Ranger turned away, pretending to be occupied with something else in order to give them a moment.

After a few seconds, Raven tapped Ranger on the arm and told him to follow her. He didn't hesitate.

Once outside she self-consciously said, "That wasn't what it seemed. I mean, kind of, but not a pity thing or something like that. I like him, but I don't think he knew it." She shrugged her shoulders.

Ranger couldn't stop himself from smiling. "And now he does."

They stood in awkward silence for a moment and then Raven said, "Let's come up with our plan of attack, shall we?"

Ranger nodded his approval, and they moved to the war tent to get to work.

Two nights later they had their plan. They were going to test the tablet messaging service. IT had found a small hole in the system they were able to exploit and could send information out from the 'head office' as it were.

Tensions were high as they all understood they would have one shot at making this work. Once their messages began scrolling across everyone's tablets, they calculated they had less than a minute to call the deputies to action before the leader or his upper-deck cronies realized none of them were originating the communications. A dash of technical skill and a heaping spoonful of luck was what they needed. They figured they had a ten-minute window to work their magic. It needed to be in-between shift changes and bathroom breaks. Any extraneous deputies and Raven's group ran the risk of the deputies telling the guards to hold until receiving confirmation.

At thirty-two minutes past midnight Ranger and Raven sat over the tablet, ready to push out their messages. They were able to schedule them to send every 7 seconds. There were four messages in total.

Ranger could feel his palms sweating. He knew his role, and he was nervous. Once the messages were sent, a main incursion team would take the building head on, weapons at the ready. Another, smaller team would distract the cadre of deputies that would be amassed in one area. Ranger was to wait until the diversion and then sneak in a side door that IT would unlock from their tablet in case the main group failed to breach the building. With his bow and arrow, he could silently infiltrate and search for the leader.

Raven took a deep breath and then pushed the button:

- Team B-3 Jameson and Greggs Rotate out T-12 minutes. Team A-5 Cooper and Carlson will report.
- Disturbance detected NE section in the forest.
- All deputies report to NE side of building. Attempted incursion. Protect

the leader.

- The leader unsafe. Moving to motorcade. Prepare for departure through NE underground garage. Deputies stay alert.

That done the head of IT corrupted all communications between the tablets. It essentially blinded both groups, but it leveled the playing field enough. At least that's what they hoped.

Everyone watched silently from the edge of the forest as each set of deputies looked down at their tablets and then at each other in confusion. A few 'is this real?' questions were heard. But their sense of duty overrode their hesitation, and they all hurried to the Northeast side of the building en masse.

Raven snapped her fingers twice and her group moved out into the open, watching for any stragglers that might sound the alarm. There was no one. Every deputy had their weapons trained on the woods, nowhere in their imaginings believing that this was an orchestrated maneuver.

As Raven's group approached the front door, still as of yet undetected, a slight thrill rushed through Ranger's body. *This might actually work*; he thought to himself. Then the first gunshot sounded.

Ranger looked up in time to see a deputy fall in front of the main entrance and Raven's team rush through the now open door of the central building. The deputies who had focused on the woods started to turn but were met with gunfire from the forest. Panic immediately set in. Some of them swung their weapons around in wide arcs, unsure if they should run back to the building, where new gunshots could be heard, or defend against the invisible shooters in the trees. Because of their indecision, a number of them were out of commission within fifteen seconds. The rest chose their battle and returned fire into the woods.

He had been so mesmerized by the whole operation that it took three nudges in his ribs to remember he had a part to play as well. The head tech looked up at him, his face sheet-white, and nodded his head toward the side door where Ranger was supposed to enter. His finger hovered over the tablet, waiting until the last second to unlock the door.

Ranger moved across the grounds, arrow nocked, sweeping the area for any rogue deputies that might have figured out what was really happening. There were none and in seconds he was at the side door. He heard shots ringing out from inside the building.

Steeling himself, Ranger reached for the door handle, twisted and pulled.

Nothing.

Nothing happened.

He tried again, panic rising into his throat.

Still nothing.

He glanced back to where the IT guys were sitting and saw them frantically tapping the screen. One of them glanced at Ranger and he registered the fear in the man's eyes. They were desperately trying to fix the problem, but it didn't seem to be working.

"Oh shit," he murmured to himself, closing his eyes, hoping the team inside was able to get through.

He leaned his head against the door and heard a soft click. Quickly he looked back at the IT guys who were all giving him enthusiastic thumbs up.

Grabbing the door handle one more time, he twisted and pulled. It opened, filling him with a combination of elation and dread. Stepping inside, he allowed the door to hit his backside so he could ease it closed without having to take his hands off the bow and arrow.

The gunfire had ceased, which made him nervous. He remembered the schematics and knew each turn to get to the main office by heart. Slowly, bowstring taut, he edged his way around a corner and glanced toward the main hall to his left. Bodies littered the floor, but it was just dark enough that he couldn't tell who had taken the brunt of the damage. He continued down the side hall and went through a small door that led to a series of anterooms. His heart felt like it was going to abandon his chest, and he tried to breathe to calm himself. He was very close to the main office and had no idea what awaited him.

A cough froze him in his steps. He waited until he heard the cough again. This time it was accompanied by a groan. The sound came from the room to his left. The door was ajar. Ranger crept over and peered inside down into the face of a man he didn't recognize. He looked up at Ranger. "Why?" the man pleaded with him, before the light went out of his eyes and his head sank to the floor with one last exhale.

Ranger swallowed the bile that had risen in his throat and made his way to the side door of the main office. Taking a deep breath, he pushed the door open and stepped through, bow at the ready.

The room was silent. His eyes swept the room and stopped on the chair behind the giant cherry wood desk. He slackened the bowstring and replaced his arrow into the quiver. Raven sat looking up at him, a smile on her face. But there was something slightly off about the smile.

Raven's left arm was clutched to her side, blood seeping between her fingers.

Stripping off his outer layer, Ranger rushed to her. He placed the balled-up clothes on the wound and told her to hold it there. She sucked a breath in through her teeth and looked as though she was about to pass out. Ranger wanted to go for help, but also knew that someone might still be alive and on the hunt.

"How bad is it?" he asked.

"Meh, I'll survive," Raven responded with a wan smile.

Ranger surveyed the room, taking stock of all the bodies. One was conspicuously missing. He turned back to Raven. "Where is he?"

She smiled again. "We are taking care of him."

Ranger took a step towards her. "What does that mean?"

"It means," she said, trying to take a deep breath. "It means that you don't need to worry about it anymore. The IT guys have sent a system-wide message telling all deputies to abandon their posts and go home. They are under the impression that the leader has been moved to a different location, and everyone is to lay low for now."

"I thought IT corrupted communications," Ranger said, puzzled.

"First rule of IT; always leave a back door."

"Huh," Ranger muttered.

Silence descended on the room, neither of them knowing what to say. Finally, Ranger decided to ask one more time, "Where is the leader?" It came out harsher than he would have liked.

Raven shook her head. "Don't do that to yourself. Don't put yourself through the anguish. Focus on the rebuild. We did what we came here to do and now we can move forward."

He opened his mouth to say something else, but Raven asked, "Are you unfulfilled?"

He thought about it.

Raven continued, "Are you upset that you weren't the one to get to him first? Are you mad you don't get to be the hero?"

Those questions were easy to answer. He simply shook his head.

"So, are you unfulfilled?" she asked again.

Ranger bit the inside of his cheek and said, "I don't think so."

"Then take the victory. Go do whatever you need to do to heal from all this. I know we have all watched the movies where the climax is some masterfully produced firefight and the tension builds and builds until finally, at the last possible moment the good guys win." Raven smiled at him. "But if I'm being honest, this was a much-preferred outcome. Sorry it wasn't more exciting."

A thought occurred to him, and he tilted his head slightly. "You sent me through the side door on purpose."

"That *was* the plan," Raven replied.

"You know what I mean," Ranger retorted.

Raven nodded. "I haven't known you for long, but I do know that I wanted your conscience to be clear. There is no reason to be haunted for the rest of your life. We have a lot of rebuilding to do and you are more of a help without fighting unnecessary demons in the middle of the night."

Ranger mulled that over in his head and then nodded. "Thank you, Raven."

She waved him off. "Aah, don't mention it."

Unsure what to do next, Ranger walked toward the main door of the office. He stopped at the threshold and Raven called after him, "Might as well take a car. The roads should be safe now."

Ranger nodded. "I'll make sure someone comes and gets you."

"Thanks," she responded. "I'm pretty sure they are on their way. One more thing, out of morbid curiosity, what are you going to do?"

Ranger thought for a moment and then answered, "There are some kids that might need me that I should get back to. Or maybe I need them. I guess we'll find out."

And with that he walked out of the central building, past what remained of the resistance group, and drove away.

THE MANY DEATHS OF JONATHAN FRAZIER

1

The first time I died it was an excruciating experience. I was hit by a car on a dark road about a mile from my house. It was rather disappointing.

Right before this, in an attempt to get healthy, I began exercising. I ramped up my stamina by walking until my lungs burned, which usually ended up being the end of the block. But eventually I progressed to two mile runs with hardly an oxygen break in the middle.

The death was unceremonious. I remember the guy who hit me kneeling beside me and spouting some garbage about calling the paramedics and for me to just stay awake. "Help is on the way!" he actually shouted at one point. All I could think of was, *Death is on the way!* But my larynx had been crushed by the direct impact it took from a very sturdy redwood, so all that came out was a gurgling wheeze, followed by a warm liquid spilling down my cheek. Judging by his horrified look, it was most likely blood. To the man's credit, he stayed by my side until I closed my eyes and all sounds faded away.

Dying is weird. I remember thinking how unfair it was. I was finally getting my life together only to have it snatched away. True, it was hard to see me on this road, even with the reflective bodysuit I was wearing. The garish outfit had saved me on multiple occasions. This stretch of road had no sidewalks and was fairly narrow for a two-way street. I had heard my share of angry epithets as motorists swerved around me at the last possible moment. I'm fairly certain I heard my guardian angel hurl a few expletives my way as well.

It probably would have been a good idea to stop running the road, but I am a creature of habit. If you were to search my house, which is what the police surely did after my demise, you would find a bedroom neatly made up with the next day's set of clothes already set out, two separate toothbrushes — one for the morning, one for the evening — and all of my food stored away in Tupperware and meticulously labeled by meal and date made. These are just a few of the things that probably scream serial killer to an outsider.

But I continued to run the road, because I have a habit of falling out of a routine and returning to old ways. Without my habitual practices, I start to believe myself when I think that the pizza I just ordered will last me a few days, as opposed to the reality of it disappearing in only a few minutes. My routines kept me on the path to health for over a year and I wasn't about to give it up due to a few near misses on a road where people really should be driving slower.

The first death was certainly unfair in my mind at the time, but after waking up from death over and over and over again I stopped being such a self-righteous prick. I mean, not right away, but eventually.

47

The 47th time I died was one of the more spectacular endings I have experienced. I actually saved a life that time. You know how in the movies the hero saves the day at the last second and everyone cheers and limps away, grateful to be alive? Picture that, except with me ending up in a gooey pile of human parts in a field near a skydiving school.

After dying forty-six times and coming back without fail, I had decided to start testing the limits of my fears, facing them head-on with reckless abandon. I figured that since I couldn't truly die, I might as well take a few risks. Skydiving was definitely near the top of my list of fears because heights were never my thing. I would always tell people that I wasn't afraid of heights, but I *was* afraid of what gravity did to things from those heights. So, I signed up for a class, which was a tandem jump. I learned how to properly equip the chute and cinch it exactly right to allow my fellas a chance to not get squeezed into oblivion.

Anyhow, then it was time to climb into the clear, blue skies and plummet back toward earth. The goal was to safely pull the cord and release the nylon strapped to our backs, allowing us to float gently to the ground, unharmed and filled to the brim with adrenaline.

The plane taxied the runway and lifted off smoothly. I found myself sitting near the back, nervously bouncing my legs up and down. My tandem partner instructor had obviously seen this behavior before. He had a big ol' grin on his face, most likely excited to scare the bejeezus out of me on the way down. Get my air legs in one giant step.

To my credit, he said I was one of the more adept newbies at putting on the chute properly. I figured he was speaking out of a different orifice than his mouth, but I secretly hoped it was true. I truly needed a confidence boost regarding this ridiculous idea. If I hadn't known about my inability to die, I would have chickened out and run from the hangar at full speed. I wouldn't have cared that I was buying an entire parachute because it was still on my back.

We reached our altitude and the instructors started yelling about preparing for the tandem jump. There were a couple frat boy types near the front of the plane that had been arrogantly bragging about how good they were at skydiving and that this was their first solo jump. Apparently, they were the best students this school, or perhaps the world, had ever seen.

One of the *boys* egged the other on, saying that he was a chickenshit and that he couldn't possibly prove his dominance in the art of skydiving unless he *unchuted* himself and put it back on before the instructors yelled for them to jump.

I'm sure you can see where this is going, but I will finish the tale.

Frat boy one unbuckles his pack and places it on the floor of the plane. Frat boy two looks around like he can't believe they were actually doing this. Both of them hoped the instructors weren't witnessing their shenanigans. And that's when the turbulence hit. It wasn't much, a slight irregularity in the air patterns, but it was enough to catch Frat boy one off guard and effectively bounce him out of the open door like a ping-pong ball, chuteless.

If I hadn't been watching their juvenile horsing around that poor Frat boy would be dead today. But because I *was* watching, and Frat boy *is* still doing whatever stupid thing he does each and every day.

Without a second thought I jumped out of the plane. My instructor had been about to buckle himself to me and hang the lead line on the wire to auto pull the chute, but I brushed past him and slipped out the door before I could even say *Yahoo!*

Frat boy was already a good couple thousand feet below me, falling toward the ground, back first. I was grateful for that because it meant he was causing resistance that slowed his descent. I made myself an aerodynamic arrow, like in the movies.

Slicing through the atmosphere I watched as Frat boy flailed and spun out of control. I could hear his screams. As I neared him, I intended to avoid his arms and legs but he had passed out. His eyes were shut, and his body had gone completely limp.

I caught one of his arms and spun him to face me, my legs wrapping around his torso as I quickly unbuckled my chute and snapped it on him. Using all the knowledge I had from the previous few hours of training, I cinched it onto his frame, not really caring about his future reproductive capabilities in the process, which became apparent when I pulled on a strap and he woke up with a start, his eyes bulging.

They always tell you not to look down, but I figured it was slightly important in order to assess how much time we had before we both became grease stains on the planet's surface. I finished my checks on the chute for Frat boy, patted him on the shoulders, realized we were too close to the ground for us to both make it if I held onto him, pulled his chute, watched him lurch upwards as the parachute deployed, and then, as he futilely reached out toward me, I waved and smiled and ten seconds later integrated my body with the hard packed earth of a field.

I am well aware I could have made some different choices, but you can judge me all you want after you have been in the same exact situation. No, I didn't think to grab his chute as I rushed out of the side of the airplane. No, I didn't try to attach him to myself while we were high enough to probably both make it safely to the ground. I was trying to think quickly, and later, after another resurrection, I checked the next day, and sure enough, Frat boy was in all the news feeds online, *like, so grateful to be alive and stuff.*

Hashtag blessed and Hashtag LuckyAF were everywhere on social media that day. People called me a guardian angel and they set up a vigil in the field near my blood smear. It was actually pretty sweet. People shared stories about their *own* guardian angels and were so grateful for the selfless acts of others. Meanwhile, I was Hashtag DeadAF as far as they were concerned, and that was a tragedy. I was cut down in the prime of my youth, so they said.

I woke up in my bed, ready to start all over again. I think I've figured out why I'm able to go around with the same name and face even after dying in front of so many people, but it's still a theory, so I'll keep it to myself for now.

112

My hero complex didn't last too long, and it ended for good after death number 112. I had taken to listening to police scanners and assisting wherever I could like some low budget Batman. A bank robbery? Let me put a stop to it. Hostage situation? Human shield. Petty thievery wasn't safe from the likes of me. Well, I mean, I basically died each time, so sometimes they definitely got away. But I never once heard about anyone else getting hurt. I counted them as wins.

Until death 112. This particular story involved saving a man from a burning, crumbling building. A fire had started in the middle of the morning due to a furnace overheating in the basement of an apartment complex. Luckily, they were able to get almost everyone out before the smoke even reached the third floor, but there was one gentleman on the fourth floor who refused to leave his home. It was explained to him what was happening, but he wouldn't budge.

This is where yours truly enters the picture. I ran up the stairs quickly, finding the man standing in his doorway. Before he could protest, I punched him hard across the face, hoping to knock him out.

One of the things I have learned through all these experiences is that movies and TV are mostly garbage when it comes to action scenes, and lovemaking, and most everything. I mean, they *are* fiction and sensationalized, so I don't blame them. It just would have been nice to have a little heads-up before I broke my hand on the man's jaw.

I watched the man's face jiggle under the blow and then he yelled some very not nice words in my general direction, so I decided to choke him out. It eventually worked and I dragged him out of the building before flames engulfed the entrance. People cheered, fire fighters clapped me on the back, and police officers told me I was stupid for going in without any training. It was a whole thing.

And then the man woke up, and his throat was throbbing. He yelled more obscenities my direction, which was just outside the building and ended it all with a threat that he was going to sue me for bodily harm and mental scarring.

Luckily, a part of the building collapsed, burying me in the rubble, but I remember thinking that I definitely didn't have the money to fight a lawsuit. And yes, I should have moved immediately away from the burning building, but the smoke inhalation had gotten to me a bit and I was more concerned with Mr. Gonna-Sue-Ya to worry about my own well-being.

One of the strange parts of this experience is that I have never seen my dead body referred to by name, not even with the skydiving incident where I signed a waiver and contract and everything. I am always unidentified. It really makes no sense, but I guess dying hundreds of times, so far, doesn't particularly fit into the natural order of things.

So, to avoid the risk of living and being sued for all I don't have, my hero complex ended right then and there. It was a shame, because I did enjoy helping people.

326

Now, I know what you're thinking. This sure is a lot of deaths, but please remember that I have not yet told you how long this had been happening. Five years to the day at death number 326. Okay, so that is still quite a few deaths, but if we are being honest, I have gone through a few phases. We could refer to them as the five stages of denied death.

Stage One: Unbelief. That stage probably lasted through about twelve or so deaths. Every time I died, I knew in my heart that it was the last one. Imagine how it felt when I came back after my ninth death and my theory that I had somehow been turned into a human cat went right out the window. Most of the deaths during this period were accidents. I was so disoriented that I didn't realize what was occurring. Death 4, walked into traffic. Death 7, walked into traffic. There wasn't a whole lot of variety in the first few.

Stage Two: Frustration. After so many deaths you really just want to die. It hurts every time, so why would I want to put myself through that over and over? Okay, so that's not entirely true. I remember feeling the pain, but my brain erases the pain when I wake up. It's sort of like going into twilight anesthesia for a wisdom tooth extraction. You know there is a memory of pain there, but your brain has blocked it out. This stage lasted for most of the double digits and included deaths such as, proving my point to a relative, and stepping off the ledge of a 20-story building. My cousin called me a coward for never doing anything slightly dangerous. I believe the actual words he used were *You are such a coward, you floss your teeth with wool.* Not the world's greatest insult, but whatever. I walked off the balcony and yelled back up at him that I was no cow… and planted myself firmly on the pavement, becoming a permanent fixture. I still see the cracked sidewalk every time I pass that building.

Side note: I have been in contact with quite a few people who have seen me die and for some reason they have a memory lapse. Maybe it's the brain's way of shutting down the trauma, but there has to be something more at play here.

Stage Three: The Hero Complex. This one ended with the aforementioned Death number 112. I probably saved close to thirty people during this stage. It felt good, and there were actually a couple times where I survived long enough to either be thanked or threatened. That was a fun stage that allowed me to live out a childhood fantasies for a while.

Stage Four: Screw It All. Death 326 falls into this stage. These deaths stand out above the rest. Depression set in hard. I mean, who wouldn't get depressed after hundreds of deaths and resurrections? I have witnessed some painful situations. And I get to remember every single one of them. I really need to figure out why I can recall my deaths and the events surrounding them, but others act as though they didn't see my brains explode all over the side of a city bus or witnessed my head being garroted off at high speed. And that's the worst thing you could do when you are depressed. Right? Not helpful.

Death 326 was a turning point for me. Curiosity overtook depression. I became what I can only describe as a homegrown scientist. I got logbooks and charts and had so many spreadsheets on my computer that it was hard to keep track of them all. You know those movies where someone is paying more attention to something they just discovered than their surroundings and they are hit by a car, sending papers flying everywhere? Count me in on that old trope. I was so pissed when I woke up, because I knew there would be no finding the papers, and I hadn't yet scanned them into my computer or backed them up.

I did find one paper, but all it said was, *The Hole Mole Rolled a Whole Vole into a Vast Crevasse.* Don't ask me what I was thinking when I wrote it. I don't have a clue. The lunatic ramblings of a budding mad scientist, I guess.

Working on trying to figure out why this phenomenon was happening to me slowly pushed the depression to the side and I became obsessed with finding answers.

Stage Five: Movies and TV. This is the stage I am currently in, which is actually quite a bit of fun. Think of it as *Mythbusters* for the immortal soul. We've all seen the movies where someone repeats the same day over and over or dies a crazy death. So, I am testing some of them out. This has been the best stage yet and I imagine it will last quite a while. Technically Death 326 fits into Stage Five as well. But I'm not one for semantics.

420

Oh wait, I was about to totally skip past two separate deaths that don't really fit any of the stages but were a lot of fun. The first one being my 420th death. Some of you are already smiling. You know what I'm about to tell you. But for the less well-informed, 420 is a number associated with marijuana. Fun fact, 420 became associated with weed culture because of a small group of California teenagers who would smoke weed at 4:20pm every day. Imagine having that iconic impact on something where you probably have to be reminded that it was you who started the whole thing.

Science says that you cannot overdose on marijuana. I wanted to try and prove Science wrong. Discover a new way to die. Here are my findings:

A) You can't technically die from overdosing on the devil's grass
B) You can become so paranoid that you forget how to breathe and run around the neighborhood asking who stole your lungs until you accidentally break into someone's house, and they defend themselves with a firearm

So, I would call the conclusion a strong maybe. You might not overdose and be announced dead based on the amount of marijuana you inhale or ingest, but you can trip balls hard enough to get yourself killed. I would not recommend it to anyone. I swear I still felt some of the effects when I woke up the next morning.

666

I'm not going to lie, I thought this was my best chance at breaking the cycle. Why not the number of the beast? I was already living in some weird, existential hell, so why not end it on the sixes?

I planned this death out to the tiniest detail. I bought black candles, a book on communing with the dead, a Ouija board I found at the local thrift store, and a dark shroud to lay over myself as I perished.

I figured, if I go to the place where I wake up every time after dying there should be some form of dimensional irony that breaks my timeline loose and makes it disappear. Or something like that.

Setting everything up in my bedroom was simple enough. I made a pentagram out of the candles and placed the Ouija board in the middle. I read up on communing with the dead as much as I could before it bored me to almost death. And then I lay down on my bed, threw the shroud over myself and called out to the unknown spirits of the universe to quicken my journey to the underworld or wherever else they might want to usher me. I swear I felt a small breeze, but it was most likely just my imagination.

When I was satisfied the spirits were listening, I reached for the rope I had attached to the candles and yanked on them, tipping the candles over and igniting the Ouija board and rug around them. I lay silently under my shroud, waiting for the flames to arrive at the bed, which they did. Science once again got things right.

As I've said before, I don't remember the feeling of burning alive, just a whisper of what the pain must have felt like. I'm sure it was excruciating at the time. And since I am relaying this story now, spoiler alert, I woke up the next morning in the ashes of my bedroom staring up at the clouds. It was fairly obvious the firefighters had been there the night before, extinguishing the blazing inferno. Everything was soggy and dripping.

I had heard that bodies take a long time to turn to ash, so I looked for my body, but when I couldn't find it, I figured the flames were too hot to leave any traces behind. Also, Satan let me down, so that was a real bummer.

Oh, also also, I'm technically homeless now.

683

And here we are. Present day. Well, the last death before present day. The day I saw *her*. Now, I am not one for kismet or meet-cutes or destiny, but when I saw her, I was drawn to her. There was a magnetism that mercilessly tugged at me, forcing me to pay attention. I mean, I even tried to leave the area and regroup, but it was almost as if she was watching me too.

It was just like any other ordinary day for me, the kind where I know fake death lurks around every corner and I could very well wake up the next morning in the lot of my old house. I was finishing setting up my latest experiment based on the classic film franchise *Final Destination*, and I found myself feeling a bit snackish. I was…am…living in the basement of my older brother, who is so busy with his career that I'm fairly certain he has forgotten I even exist. I'm like some sort of squatter with bathroom privileges.

I left the basement via my private entrance and walked down to the local five and dime. As I entered, I saw her. At first it felt like a bolt of electricity had passed through my body, something I had experienced before, except this was more of the lightning variety. Then there was a low hum that got louder the closer I got to her.

I bought my snacks and left, walking back toward my brother's house. I don't know why she stuck out so prominently in my mind. Sure, I'm attracted to females, and yes, she was attractive to me. But, other than the hum, there was nothing spectacular about our little encounter.

Instead of heading back home right away, I made a detour to the local gas station. I had gotten into the habit of purchasing lotto tickets when I had extra funds, and I was sitting on a Jackson that was itching to win me a little extra cash.

I had a decent job that paid me a living wage, and I tried to keep my deaths from coinciding with my work schedule, but on occasion I had died on my way to work or during a lunch break. Things always got real awkward the next day when I had to take a tongue-lashing being told that I couldn't simply skip out on work and shirk my responsibilities. I think the only reason they keep me on is because I actually do work hard and I'm smart enough to come up with a helpful idea once in a while.

I entered the little mini mart and walked up to the counter, requesting twenty of their finest scratchers. The clerk rolled his eyes and ripped off the tickets from the roll. I had a good feeling about these. I was even willing to bet one of them held a thousand bucks under its surface.

When I turned around, I almost ran right into her. We both laughed awkwardly, and I apologized. She smiled sheepishly at me. Looking over her shoulder and through the window I could see a car careening down the street, headed straight for the gas pumps. My first thought was to get everyone to safety, but there was no time. I yelled out for everyone in the store to move toward the back of the building, but a second later an explosion rattled the glass before it shattered and a fireball came hurtling through the broken windows, which was the car the person had been driving.

I turned to shield the girl, but she just sort of stood there, like this was perfectly normal. A moment later the car hit both of us and I witnessed my first person, outside of myself, die in front of me. I had always tried to be so careful, but somewhere in the back of my mind I knew human casualties were eventually inevitable.

It had been nearly a year since my last death, and I was beginning to enjoy actually falling asleep each night. Sure, I had been setting up a new experiment, but had decided I would only pull the trigger on that if I got super bored one day and had nothing better to do.

ONE

I woke up and my first thought was that something didn't feel right. Usually when I woke up in the empty lot of my old house there was a bit of a draft, but this felt different. No breeze. No birds chirping. And the air smelled like lavender and cinnamon. That was definitely not the same.

That's when the screaming began. From right next to me. My first thought was that someone had seen me rematerialize and it had broken their brain, but then the hitting began. Fists pounded my body while the screaming continued. I opened my eyes to see some feral creature attacking me with all the strength it had. Hair swirled around my face, getting in my mouth, stinging my eyes, and all I could do was lay there and take the beating. I knew that if this continued I would eventually die at the hands of whatever H.G. Wellsian type creature was pounding on me, and simply start over the next morning.

The blows began to dissipate, and the creature shoved me one last time before backing up across the room. The room? I was in a room. There hadn't been a room last time I had reacquainted myself with this mortal soil. The creature breathed heavily, and I feared another attack was forthcoming, so I raised my hands and yelled, "Peace be unto thee!" I didn't know if this creature spoke English, but in the moment I didn't know what else to do.

Looking around the room I saw a desk, a chair, a dresser, and a door leading to a bathroom. It was a smartly decorated space. This was now someone's room. And I had just materialized out of nowhere, right in bed with them. Not a creature, a human, standing in the corner, hair cascading over their face, and a wild look in their eyes. Again, I raised my hands and stated, "I mean you no harm." The cliché passed through my lips before I could even cringe.

The human brushed the hair back from their eyes and I saw that it was a woman. A female with a book in her hand, poised to throw it at me. "Who the hell are you?"

"My name is Jonathan. Jonathan Frazier. I used to live here." My eyes were glued to the book, ready to duck if she felt the need to let loose and fling it in my direction.

The female's arm wavered for a second, but then she reared back and asked, "Why are you in my room, perv?"

"I'm not a…" I stopped and looked at her and then looked down at myself. I was fully clothed. Pajama bottoms and a thin t-shirt. Just had to make sure. "Okay, listen. I can explain what is happening, but you might not believe me."

"Sounds like something a perv would say," she retorted.

I finally got a good look at her and cocked my head to one side. I tried not to smile, but I couldn't stop it. "You were in the gas station yesterday. Where the explosion happened."

I saw panic in her eyes as she tried to think of a rational response and what she said was hilarious and a little cute. "Yeah? So? I…escaped out the back before the explosion. I'm psychic."

My guard was now fully down, and the smile had turned to a large grin. "Psychic? Then why did you let all those people die?"

Her face turned beet red, and she stammered, "I…but…I didn't…I'm not a very good psychic."

"Okay, let's go with that." I let the silence marinate for a few seconds before continuing. "Now for the real story. You and I both died in that fiery inferno that came shooting through the front windows."

A flicker of comprehension in her eyes before she went back into full denial mode. "That's impossible. You can't come back from the dead. That's not how it works."

"Okay, Romero, but I *know* for a fact that *I* died. And I'm fairly certain

I was trying to shield you from the blast when it hit. So, either we both have the same superpower, or I need to see a psychiatrist." I looked at her with a bit of defiance.

Finally, she slumped her shoulders and let the book fall to the floor. "Fine."

That was it? *Fine?* Not even a *holy crap we are in the same boat and now we have someone else to talk to about this and what the actual eff is going on with us to the point where we can never die!!!?*

I was now freaking out on the inside. I wanted to run up and hug her and sit and talk for ages about everything. But she was clearly unimpressed by the whole situation. Fine. Sweet Lord on high.

She continued to stare at me, and the look told me she was starting to get annoyed. "So, you just gonna stand in my room, or…" Her eyes flicked toward the door.

"In a minute. Can I ask one question?" I thought for a second. "I mean, besides that question, of course." I felt like an awkward teenager talking to a girl for the first time. I was nervous and amazed.

"Fine," she replied without emotion.

Fine. Today's resurrection brought to you by the word *fine.* "How many times?"

"How many times what?" Her annoyance hid something else. Curiosity, maybe?

"Have you died? Obviously, it isn't your first or you'd be all like, 'Holy crap, what the hell, how am I even here right now?' So, how many times have you died?" I raised my eyebrows in anticipation.

"I don't know. I don't keep track." I should have seen that response coming, but I was too excited. I needed to temper my expectations a bit.

"You…you don't keep track? Why not?" I felt like I was edging back into book toss territory, but I couldn't help myself.

"That's another question. How many times have you died?" she asked with a perfect snarky pitch.

"That would total six-hundred-eighty-three times," I proclaimed, with a slight bow.

"Bullshit." Monotone response.

"No shit." Attempt at hiding excitement response.

I saw a break in her icy cold exterior and took it as a good sign. "That's crazy. I think I'm around twelve or something."

She moved and sat on her bed, and I stayed precisely where I was. "I know I've reached my quota for questions, but may I ask your name?"

Her shoulders slumped and she kind of melted her body onto her bed, grabbing her pillow and holding onto it. "Chloe. And go ahead and ask."

I sat down on the ground and smiled at her. "Chloe. That's a great name. I'm sorry you're stuck not dying. It took me a while to get used to it too. It's kind of the best and worst thing ever."

"Emphasis on worst," she replied softly.

I was still reeling from the revelation of another immortal. "So, Chloe, what do you want to know?"

She shrugged her shoulders. "What's the worst way you've died?"

I proceeded to tell her about a few different incidents where the pain was unbearable, and I probably should have read the social cues, because by the time I was done with my tellings, she looked as though she wanted to live in a bubble and protect herself in any way possible. "I mean, the really painful deaths are few and far between." And then another thought struck me. "I mean, I'm not out here trying to die all the time. Like, well, okay, I *have* tried to die in different ways, but only as scientific experiments. But it's only because I know I can't die."

"And what happens if you are wrong just one time?" She had sat on her bed and started to look interested in the conversation for the first time since she tried to pound the life out of me.

"If I'm wrong, I guess that's that. I don't have to worry about it anymore. But after nearly 700 deaths I've kind of become estranged to the thought of permanence." I really thought about what I was saying and realized that it was actually kind of a sad existence. Maybe that's why I had stopped most of my experimentation and was simply living my life now. As I said before, I hadn't died in nearly a year.

"How long have you been dying?"

The question was simple enough, but I still found myself laughing. Any other circumstance and that question would have been a somber request for information. But here, in this room, it was borderline absurd. "Over six years now." I did quick math in my head. "I've died around a hundred times a year. Hmmm…that's wild."

"That's a long time. But I guess time doesn't really matter anymore." Frustration bit into her voice again.

I knew the stage all too well. Pissed off, sad, hating the fact that I couldn't die permanently. She would get over it, but it could take a while. "What happened the first time you died?" I asked, attempting to ground the conversation.

She shrugged her shoulders again. "Not much to tell. I was out with some friends. A drunk driver hit us with his car. They all lived, but I didn't make it. I woke up in my bed like it had never happened. I wasn't sore, nothing was broken, I was fine." She stopped for a second, a faraway look entering her eyes. "You wanna know the weirdest part?"

"Everyone acted as if nothing had ever happened." That wasn't quite right. "Well, it happened, but no one remembered that you died. Business as usual."

She nodded. "I went up to my friend Trish and asked her about the accident and she told me she was so glad I wasn't in the car, because the empty seat was where the impact occurred, and I would have been toast." She scrunched up her eyebrows. "She didn't even remember I had gone out with them in the first place."

"Did you try to correct her?" I asked, genuinely curious to have another perspective on this unique experience.

"I thought it best I didn't. I don't think anything I could have said would've changed her mind." She bit the inside of her lip.

The mood was dropping into melancholy territory, so I clapped my hands together, startling Chloe, and told her we should go get something to eat. That would cheer us both up and then we could talk about next steps. She looked at me like she would rather eat a cactus but stood up anyhow.

I looked at her bed and realized she had a Queen size. Maybe that was why we didn't end up in a pile when we came back. The bed is bigger, so maybe she slept in a slightly different spot than I did? That seemed like thin logic, at best.

Then I started imagining what if a lot of people started coming back and we all died at the same time and ended up in a giant dog pile and had to untangle ourselves. Or Chloe didn't die for a long while and randomly some mornings a different person would be on her bed with her. That would be hilarious. Chloe cleared her throat and brought me back to the room. "Right. Food. Shall we?"

We walked out of her room, and I couldn't help but gawk at the new house that stood where the desiccated corpse of my old house once did. "I think it bears mentioning that I used to live here."

She stopped dead in her tracks, and I nearly ran into her back. "You used to *live* here? When? This house was just completed this last year."

"Oh, before. The original house burned down." I paused. "I burned it down." She looked at me with a judgy expression on her face. "It was an experiment. I thought I would actually die if I did that." I raised my hands in defeat. "Guess I was wrong."

She stared at me for a long moment, and it got super awkward, at least for me, and then she turned and walked out of the house.

TWO

We ended up at a little taco joint that Chloe swore by. She was starting to loosen up a bit, which was nice. She could pack away some tacos. I was aware of how hungry resurrection could make a person. I did my fair share of taco chomping as we got to talking about next steps. She liked the idea of experimenting, and I loved the idea of being able to test my hypotheses with another person.

"Okay," she said, between a mouthful of crunchy beef taco. "So, we've established that we both have lived in that house."

"Yes." I nodded.

"And we both slept in that same room."

"Uh huh."

"And when we die, we return to that spot, sort of like a respawn zone."

"True."

She rolled her eyes. "I'm just thinking out loud. You don't have to respond after every statement."

"Sorry. Excited." Then as an afterthought I added, "Continue."

"Okay, so there must be something with that house. Or spot, more appropriately."

As she talked, I realized that I was falling for her. Not...you know...physically. Although, she was incredibly attractive, but intellectually. The way her mind worked melded with my approach to this situation. It was like a match made in a beaker in someone's lab.

"What if we research the plot of land where we both respawn and see if there is any odd connection to why this might be happening?"

I stayed silent, still abiding by the not responding to every statement concept, not realizing she had actually asked me a question this time.

"Dude, this is not rhetorical. What do you think?"

My brain doubled back to make sure I remembered the question correctly and then I nodded and said, "Yes." That's it. Nothing more. I must have sounded like an idiot. So, I elaborated. "Yes. That sounds like a great plan to research the plot of land where we both respawn." So, maybe I overelaborated.

I still got a small giggle out of her, which made me smile. I really needed to get a handle on myself. I had become so methodical over the last few years, and it was all falling apart in my mind like silly string.

Taking a deep breath, and a bite of delicious taco, I thought of something I wanted to test out. "Okay, we research the plot of land, and in the meantime, we can try and figure out why everyone forgets about us when we die."

"And how are we supposed to do that, exactly?"

I smiled. "One of us dies while the other one watches." The smile died. "I mean, that sounds super creepy or whatever. But seriously, if we are in the same spot and one of us dies while the other is in the area, maybe we can figure out some clue as to why no one ever remembers our dead faces." I shut my mouth.

Chloe nodded. "Yeah. That could work. So, how do you want to die?"

I narrowed my eyes. "Now, wait a minute. I've died so many times and I had meticulous notes and equations and diagrams on notepads for years and you are going to come in and think you will be the observer?"

She set her taco down and looked me square in the eyes and said, "Yep."

We had a little stare down. I wasn't about to give up that easily. So, I leaned in real close and said, "Well, I think something simple should do the trick. But I want it to be public enough for you to gauge the reaction of those around you. Any thoughts?"

She took a bite of taco and chewed, contemplating ideas. "I could shoot you."

I tilted my head. "You could. But what if everyone remembers enough to know that you murdered someone and then there is a whole investigation, and you're put on trial, sending you to prison?"

"I just die and reset."

"Okay, but what a waste."

"Okay, but what a thrill."

"Perhaps another time. I think we should start simple, maybe a little less murdery, and work our way up to…murder."

"Fine." I was beginning to suspect that was her favorite word.

"Let me think on it and I'll get back to you. We could probably make tomorrow work." I spoke with the confidence of a man who didn't have a job. "Hold up, I have work tomorrow. It might have to wait a couple days."

"There's a good question. How do you keep your job when you die and can't show up for a shift?" It truly was weird having a conversation of this nature with another person. We weren't even keeping our voices down or anything.

"Well, I try to keep my deaths to a minimum, but if I really must die, I try to do it on my off days. Luckily, I am fairly unsupervised, and I do a good enough job that if I miss a day here or there they don't really complain." I shrugged my shoulders. "Besides, I haven't died in nearly a year, so my attendance record has been impeccable."

Chloe nodded her head. "That makes sense. So far, I haven't died at an inconvenient time. I would call that a win."

"Definitely a win." I brushed my hands off on a napkin and wiped my face. "What do you want to do with the rest of the day?"

She looked at me with wide eyes and awkwardly smiled. "I have work in a couple hours. So, I'm gonna go do that."

The redness crept up my cheeks. I didn't have to see it to know it was true; I could feel the heat rising into my face. "Yeah, of course you do. I think we should at least exchange numbers so we can keep in touch. Meet back up with our findings when we have a chance. Conduct our little experiment. Get some more tacos."

We exchanged phone numbers and said our farewells and it took me three tries to figure out which way I needed to go to get to the library. Anyone who may have been watching me probably got a good little comedy show. And I realized, of all the ways I have died, embarrassment wasn't one of them.

Yet.

THREE

The library. The library. The library library library. I have always hated the library. And, before you get all offended and in a huff, it has nothing to do with the idea of gaining knowledge or the invaluable resource that it truly is. My issue is the Dewey Decimal System. I just can't figure it out. So, instead of being able to find whatever it is I'm looking for, I peruse the aisles for about 45 minutes until I give up and leave.

But this time I had a mission, and I was bound and determined to find a librarian who knew exactly where to find information on the history of the town.

I spotted her as soon as I entered the building. My hands started to sweat. There was something about the librarian that made me uncomfortable. Maybe it had to do with the authority they wielded in keeping people quiet, distributing knowledge, and having the ability to kick people out for being disruptive.

Approaching the desk, I almost chickened out and walked up to the 'New in Library' section that held a mishmash of fiction and non-fiction and even a few Blu-Rays. But then she looked up and smiled and I knew I couldn't simply pass her by.

I stepped up to the desk and rapped my knuckles on the Formica countertop. Immediately regretting my decision, I rubbed the counter, as if in an attempt to apologize to the inanimate object for hitting it. I let out a small, awkward laugh and tried to smile at the librarian. She had begun to look a bit nervous.

Glancing at her nametag I cleared my throat and in a too loud whisper said, "Hi Mabel, I was wondering if you could help me."

She winced at the harsh, grunting whisper, but turned on a welcoming smile and leaned in a bit. "What can I help you with, dear?"

"Yes, hi, I was wondering about books on the history of this town? Maybe old maps, or I don't know, something, anything to help me know…history." I was actually proud of myself for not passing out.

Mabel seemed far less impressed.

She glanced over my shoulder and tilted her head slightly. I turned to look and there directly behind me was a giant display that had a sign that read: INTERESTED IN THE HISTORY OF OUR LITTLE TOWN? START HERE!

And, yes, it was all in caps. And, also yes, I found it ironic for a sign in a library to be yelling at me.

The next thing that happened I am not proud of, and I'm only repeating it here for the sake of posterity. I put my finger to my lips, and I shushed the sign. If you feel that perhaps it wasn't cringey enough, I then turned to Mabel, the ever-patient librarian, and said, with a smirk on my face, "The sign was yelling at me. It should know it's in a library."

They say you go through your most awkward phases as a teenager. I am here to report to you that that is wildly inaccurate. Maybe some people go through their awkward stage as a teenager, but I am a life-long member. Kind of wished I had the ability to literally die from embarrassment. But, alas, there I stood, in broad daylight, staring at a librarian named Mabel, who was looking back at me with zero amusement on her face.

Then a funny thing happened. Mabel stood up and leaned in close to me, shaking her head. I thought for sure I was going to be banned for making such a stupid joke and braced myself for the news. "I told Charlie we were going to have to deal with that joke if he put the sign in all caps with an exclamation at the end. But, oh no, Charlie doesn't want to listen. I think he likes to torture me." And she sat back down in her seat, the chair letting out a *WHOOMPF* of air that somehow sounded like it agreed with her.

She began typing and then realized I was still standing there and asked,

"Anything else I can help you with, dear?"

All I could do was shake my head and turn toward the yelling display, picking up books, replacing them, making sure they were set down perfectly. I could feel Mabel's eyes on me, but I tried to act nonchalant.

A display tends to serve more than one purpose. The first, and most obvious purpose is to show off the wares to entice people to look at them and either purchase or borrow the items. The second, and far more sinister purpose is to humiliate people like me. As I set one of the books back into its stand, the stand snapped, causing the book to tumble, which created a chain reaction of other books on the display being tipped over and pamphlets spilling onto the floor. By the time the Rube-Goldberg machine had finished its little dance, one book remained on the display and all the rest were looking up at me pathetically from the carpet.

I turned to Mabel, who was no longer in a forgiving mood, and whispered, "I'll check them all out, please."

Mabel's nostrils flared, and I could tell she was trying really hard not to break the code of near silence of the sacred library, but I could also see the vein bulging to near popping that pulsated on her forehead. Either I was going to escape this lion's den by the skin of my teeth, or this was going to be death 684.

To give myself the slightest chance of leaving the library with all my limbs intact I began scooping up all the pamphlets that had rejoiced in being freed from their stand, by spreading as far and wide as they could reach. I tried not to crumple the papers, but if you couldn't tell at this point in the story, I'm. Not. A. Smooth. Operator.

Five minutes later, crumpled pamphlets shoved hastily back in their plastic stand, twelve books in my arms, and sweat glistening on my forehead, I approached Mabel once again. She had watched the entire situation and hadn't offered to assist me in any way. I don't blame her.

I plopped the books down on the counter and pointed at them. Mabel closed her eyes, took a deep breath, and stated, "You can only check out five books at a time." She had abandoned calling me 'dear'. This was worse than I thought. And now I would have to sit and sift through these books to find five that would hopefully be of the most help to me in my quest.

In the end I simply went with the five books that were on the top of the pile. I needed to get out of there, and making more decisions seemed like the poorest decision.

I handed the books and my library card to Mabel, she scanned them through, and then I left without so much as a single utterance.

FOUR

Back at home, I finally felt as though I could breathe normally again, and now, with a can of soda in front of me, and the books on my desk, I was ready to delve into some history.

As I sorted through the books a couple of them had promise, but two of them had to do with historical cuisine and one was essentially about the dialect and how it came to be.

The two that interested me were about local landmarks and town folklore. Since I couldn't really explain why I wasn't allowed to die, I figured folklore might possibly provide some options to bring to my next meeting with Chloe.

I opened the book about landmarks and when I woke up three hours later, I was still on page xxi of the introduction. This was going to be a lot more strenuous than I had anticipated. I upgraded my soda to an energy drink and got back to it.

Despite the dryness of the text, which held such gems as: *As far back as 1847 the plot of land that encompasses the national forest was always known for its indigenous species such as deer, bobcats, and even hedgehogs,* there were some tidbits that were quite fascinating. Sonic roaming the woods aside, I discovered that most of the buildings that stood in town were originals. There were the obvious exceptions of newer townhomes and condos that had popped up over the last twenty years or so. The book had been published about twenty-five years prior, and I knew my house was an original. Until I burned it down, of course.

The town was established in 1847, hence the eponymous plot of land with bobcats and hedgehogs. Originally, it was intended to be only a temporary stopping point for a group of pioneers. They were headed across the country to join in the gold rush in California, but too many of them died along the way, so they holed up here in an attempt to repopulate and heal. They fell in love with the place, naming it Cinder Falls, even though there were no known waterfalls in the area, and over the years developed it into a thriving community.

By 1897 they had built close to one-hundred homes and had a population of 362 people. In 1937, a few years before World War II, they established a historical society. The men and women of this society got a map of the boundaries of Cinder Falls and went acre by acre determining what various landmarks they should have.

There was the town's oldest oak tree, which I walked by at least three times a week. The oldest building stood in the outskirts of town and had been turned into a museum to show visitors the history and growth of the community.

If you look closely, you will see the piece of parchment that was used as a crude representation of the boundary lines of Cinder Falls when it was first established.

The audio guided tour was something to hear, for sure. Interestingly enough, and I only knew this because my parents told me when I built my little house, but no one had ever erected anything on that plot of land up until I did.

Before you go off thinking I'm some secret rich guy, the land was dirt cheap, the materials were inexpensive, and the house was a one-bedroom, 800 square foot job. I happen to be handy with tools and did most of the building myself. Anything structural I hired a guy, but most everything else was all me.

I thought it was probably nothing, but maybe I erected my house unknowingly on an ancient burial ground and the ghosts were all like, *hey, let's mess with this fella. Make it so he can't die.* Yeah, it doesn't seem like a highly likely scenario to me either.

Nonetheless, I figured I might as well check if that land had any weird origins, like a grave site, just in case.

I was getting bored reading about the history of this sleepy little town and figured it was time to go get something to eat, maybe some more caffeine as well.

I wondered what Chloe was up to and if she had made any discoveries of her own. Two days until I got to die again. It *was* really weird waking up in someone else's bed.

I stood up, stretched, popped my neck, which felt amazing, and headed out the door. I was feeling pizza. Anchovies and pepperoni. Yeah.

FIVE

When you have died as many times as I have and inevitably come back, you start to ignore your surroundings. When danger is removed, apathy settles in. Not with all things, but with important, life-saving things. Such as, watch out for the other driver, because they aren't watching out for you. Or look both ways before you cross the street. That's a big one.

Long story short, I didn't heed the wisdom of looking as I went to get my pizza. The car was fancy, but I didn't have enough time to see exactly what kind it was before I was sent cartwheeling into the air.

My last thought as I landed on the pavement and had the wind knocked out of me was, *I don't remember leaving my shoes over there. How strange.*

SIX

I woke up to screaming again. It took me a moment, and then I braced for impact, which came seconds later. Chloe wasn't super strong, so I lay there with my eyes closed and took the beating.

Eventually the hits stopped coming and I opened one eye to see where Chloe might be. She was frantically putting on a shirt and so I squeezed my eye shut once again. I could hear her breathing heavily.

"What the hell, Jonathan?" she finally intoned. Judging by the sound of her voice she was still across the room.

Without opening my eyes, I responded, "I didn't mean to. I was hit while crossing the road. It was an accident."

A long silence then, "Did you look both ways?"

"Ummm," I replied with great confidence.

"Dude," she replied quickly. Then, "Did you see me without my shirt on?"

"Nope. Promise. I kept my eyes closed." I pointed at my eyes. "See? Still closed."

Chloe let out a long breath and said, "You can open your eyes now. I'm dressed. I guess I don't get to sleep without a nightgown on anymore. That sucks."

I raised an eyebrow, amused. "Nightgown? Do you have a small candle you take to bed so you can see where you're headed?"

Chloe was *not* amused. "Har har. Laugh it up. Pajamas. I have to wear actual pajamas now."

I stood up from the bed and smiled. I may have been enjoying myself a bit too much. "Don't let my random drop-ins stop you. You do your thing."

Chloe opened her mouth to issue a retort, but then the expression on her face changed and she pushed out her lower lip. She was thinking about something. I let her sit with her thoughts until she blurted, "What were you wearing when you died?"

I looked down at myself and saw I was wearing pajama bottoms and a thin t-shirt. "Not this. I think that whatever happens, a cloning process or whatever, it accounts for the items of clothing you were wearing the morning of your death."

Chloe looked skeptical. I couldn't blame her. "I don't know if it's some sort of scanning mechanism or what it is, but this is what I was wearing the last time I slept in my room. Since I don't sleep in my room, this room, anymore I guess I'm destined to wake up wearing the same pajama bottoms and t-shirt."

Finally, Chloe looked at ease and stated, "Sounds like you're grasping at straws."

I shrugged. "Probably. I'm going off of pure experience with zero factual findings. That's why I started writing everything down and trying to figure out what was happening from a scientific angle. But, if I'm being honest, I'm not smart enough to figure it out."

Chloe looked at me and feigned shock. "You know, I have a friend who works in a lab at the community college. He may not be top brass in his field, but he is quite intelligent. Maybe we could talk to him about it."

I thought about it for a second. "Why don't we try our little experiment first and see how that goes. Then we can talk about telling your boyfriend."

"I didn't say boyfriend."

"Well, that's good, because we keep waking up in bed together and that could drive a wedge between you and him."

"You're just a twelve-year-old in a grown man's body, aren't you?"

I raised my hands in defeat. "You got me. I'm Tom Hanks in the movie *Big.*"

Chloe smiled. "So, this little trial run we're planning, I think I've had enough scares for the week. Why don't *I* die, and you chart the results?"

I honestly hadn't expected this, so instead of responding verbally, I nodded my head. A lot. Like, way too much head nodding.

"Okay, don't get too excited to kill me off," she said, a playful tone in her voice.

"Have you thought of a way to go? How you wanna off yourself?" The corners of my lips turned down. "Sorry, I didn't mean to sound so…flippant."

Chloe shook her head. "I get it. And yeah, I think poison is the best route. Something that will act fast, make it a swift death."

I looked at her, skepticism filling my face, "And you have access to said poisons?"

"I told you I know a guy who works at the community college. He has stuff in his lab that'd kill a rhino."

"But we agreed to not involve him."

"He won't know."

I was beginning to like this scenario less and less. But what else were we going to do? "Okay, fine. Just don't get caught. Pick your poison and get out of there."

Chloe laughed. "You can't help yourself, can you?"

I was confused. "What?"

"Pick your poison?"

Since I am writing this all down for posterity, I will be completely honest when I say that it took me far too long to connect the phrase to the conversation, and by the time I did Chloe had moved on to something else completely. But don't worry, dear reader, I brought it back with all the awkward energy I could muster.

Chloe was in the middle of explaining her relationship with scientist whatshisname and I blurted out, "Oh yeah, like the phrase."

Now it was Chloe's turn to be confused, but she caught on a lot quicker than I did. "Living in the past, are we? Catch up. We have some planning to do."

It was the nicest way anyone has ever pulled me out of being awkward. It felt like she didn't care that I had interrupted the flow of conversation and acted as if it weren't awkward at all. I had grown so accustomed to friends and family taking a moment of my awkwardness and stretching it like taffy until I broke. Now, in this moment, I wasn't quite sure what to do. So, I tried to shove my hands in my pajama bottom's pockets and realized too late that they did not in fact have pockets and said, "We want to do this in public, right?"

Chloe paused for a second, smiled sweetly at me, and then continued, "Yes. The more people that are around when it happens the more reactions you will be able to pull from. And then we'll meet up the next morning to discuss your findings."

I exhaled slowly. "That sounds good to me. So, tomorrow we will go somewhere public, you will ingest poison, myself and a bunch of other people will watch you die, and then we get some coffee and chit-chat."

"Precisely," Chloe responded with a nod.

We stood in uncomfortable silence for a long moment before I cleared my throat and said, "I'm off to work. I will see you tomorrow."

"See you tomorrow, Jonathan."

I walked out of her room and let myself out of the house and headed to my brother's basement to get ready for work.

SEVEN

The warehouse seemed particularly empty as I clocked in for my job. I knew my buddy Earl would be setting up the pallet jacks for when the trucks arrived. He was one of those go-get-'em one step ahead of everyone else guys. And don't get me wrong, I work hard at my job, but I also don't work hard enough to be noticed. There is a sweet spot right in the middle where I get to exist by doing just the right amount of work.

I walked the floor, but I didn't see any pallet jacks set up at the bay doors. In fact, I didn't see anyone at all. The hell? The place was usually bustling with activity, but I swear you could hear a mouse fart in this place.

I figured I could simply go to the break room, toss my lunch in the refrigerator and get to work. As I passed the last truck bay, I thought I heard someone sniffling, but I shook my head and threw open the door to the break room. A cacophony of *Surprise!!!* met my ears and I thought for a second, I was going to have a heart attack.

The break room was stuffed to the brim with my coworkers. After I came down from my adrenaline high, they informed me they had all chipped in together to get me a gift card and a cake to celebrate my one-year anniversary of working with them. Of course, most of them made sure to mention how lucky I was to be able to work with them. Hardy har har and a slap on the back before heading out onto the floor. I humored them and once everyone had left except me and Earl, I looked at the gift card. It was to a restaurant that most of the crew absolutely loved, but had given me…problems, on multiple occasions.

I saw the look on Earl's face, and I spun it through the air to him. "Enjoy yourself, buddy. Looks like there's about a hundred bucks on it. That'll buy you all the intestinal distress you could ever desire."

To his credit, Earl snatched that card out of the air and pocketed it in one swift motion. "Thanks. I will put it to good use. Dolores and I have been seeing each other for a while. I'm gonna take her out on a nice date."

I did a double take. "Dolores? Like, old lady Dolores? Like, adjusts her wig every five minutes Dolores?"

Earl took a step toward me. "Hey, don't talk about my lady that way."

I held my hands up in defense. "No, no. I was just wondering how you could land such a vixen. That's all."

Earl took another step toward me. "Back off, buddy. We might be friends, but that doesn't mean you get to steal my woman."

Perhaps I should explain a bit about Earl. I met Earl when I first started working at this job. He decided to take me under his wing and show me the ropes. Mind you, he is about ten years my junior, and it takes him a bit of time to process information. I love the guy to bits, but he can be a bit slow when it comes to sarcasm or joking around. I never fault the man for it, and to be honest, I take a bit of advantage in harmless ways. Such as the conversation we were currently having.

"I would never dream of stealing your girlfriend. You mean too much to me to do that. I hope you both have a long and wonderful relationship. I will await the wedding invitation with bated breath." I smiled at Earl.

He walked past me and clapped me on the shoulder. "You might not want to bait your breath. We are taking things real slow."

I turned and followed him out of the room. "That's probably a wise decision. Make sure it's for real."

Earl shrugged. "Exactly. You get me, my young Padawan. Maybe some day I will teach you the ways of the master."

We got to work and to be honest I sort of zoned out for most of the shift. Until we were nearing the conclusion of our time. Earl was chatting up his girlfriend Dolores, who was busily adjusting her wig and I heard her say, "I was up in my apartment, and I saw the whole thing happen. Your buddy was hit by a car, and he died on the pavement."

Earl shook his head and chuckled. "But he is literally ten feet away. Like, right now. Look." He gestured at me.

"I know. I can see him. But I'm telling you, it happened yesterday. He died and then his body just disintegrated."

Earl looked over at me and saw I was staring right at the two of them and he scoffed and shrugged. "I don't know what to tell you, man. Apparently, you're dead."

I know discretion should have been the go-to move, but I was too intrigued by the fact that someone actually remembered seeing me die. I wanted to pick her brain, but I thought I would start off simple. "Are you sure it was me?" I asked, hoping I didn't sound too eager.

She nodded her head confidently. "Oh yeah. I was watering my azaleas and I happened to look down and see you exit a basement. I didn't really think much of it until I heard the car screech and I looked up from my watering and saw you tumble across the street."

"And I just stayed on the street? You didn't see me get up?" I moved over closer to them and grabbed a chair.

"Nope. The driver got out of his car, but he looked confused. By the time I looked back at your body, it was gone."

Earl looked thoroughly confused. "So, you *did* see him get up."

Dolores hit Earl on the arm. "Earl, why don't you listen? He didn't get up. Unless he left all his clothes in the middle of the road."

All I could think about was that poor driver getting out of his car and wondering why he stopped in the first place. And then wondering why someone would throw clothes into the middle of the street. I must have been smiling, because both Earl and Dolores were looking at me like I had told them to take a flying leap.

"Sorry, I was just thinking about what you might have seen. I mean, do you think I'm a zombie or something? Only person I know who pulled off the feat of coming back from the dead was—"

"Neo," Earl interrupted.

I couldn't help but smile. "Sure, Earl. Neo. And he's a fictional character."

Dolores looked at me, suspicion growing every second. "I know what I saw, young man. Do not confuse me with some old doddering geriatric."

I actually scooted my chair back a few inches. The intensity with which she spoke was quite impressive. "Never, Miss Dolores. Never."

Earl made a motion with his eyes to let me know I was upsetting Dolores and I stood from the chair and said, "I think I am going to call it a night. Go get a good night's rest. I will see you all in a few days for my next shift."

Dolores glared at me, and Earl turned to her to console her. With his off hand he made a shooing gesture and that is precisely what I did.

EIGHT

Chloe had texted me early in the morning letting me know where she wanted to meet and at what time. I was overly excited to tell her about the conversation I had the night before with my coworkers. Someone had actually witnessed me die and remembered enough to be frightened of me. Okay, so the frightened bit wasn't the cool bit. Nonetheless, it was something to be checked into further.

I stood near the entrance of the outlet mall that was a few miles from my place. She told me she would meet me at a quarter to six. That way all the stores would still be open and most people who worked the nine to five would have gotten a chance to go shopping or go out to eat. It made sense to me, and to be honest, if Chloe had suggested we climb up a mountain and scream for everyone to look, I probably would have agreed to it, because I was in such a darn good mood.

There were people milling about everywhere. This was going to be the perfect experiment. I looked at my watch and saw it was almost seven and I still hadn't heard back from her. With how many people were actually here I wasn't super surprised, but I figured she would at least be on time for something this important. Finally, I saw someone that looked like Chloe, but as she got closer, I realized that it was a guy with longer hair.

I turned away just in case he saw the pretend look of recognition in my eyes, and someone bumped into me. I mean, I guess it was someone, because I felt myself sway, but when I turned around, I was standing near the fountain at the center of the mall. And no one was near me.

It wasn't like me to wander freely, but I guess I did have a lot on my mind. I wondered if I had missed Chloe, so I checked my cell phone. No new messages. Now I was getting a little annoyed. I sent her a scathing text about how I was left stranded, looking like an idiot and blah blah blah. I really laid it on thick. And I hit send before I could be less emotional about the situation.

After I sent a new text apologizing for my tone in the previous text, I sent a third text asking very politely where she could be instead of helping test our hypothesis. I looked at my phone waiting for the little wiggling dots to appear, but none did. Great, I may have lost my lab partner. And new friend.

The whole drive home I stressed about the way I sounded on the texts. I figured I should probably send her one more, just so she knew I wasn't really upset, simply super excited. That's all. But, no, that was probably overkill. I chuckled to myself at the situational pun.

I only checked my phone a million more times on my drive home, but by the time I went to bed for the night she still hadn't responded. Maybe she had accidentally died on the way to meet me. That is definitely possible. I mean, I was hit by a car two days ago, completely an accident, so there was a chance something like that had happened to Chloe.

Either way I had calmed myself down enough by the time I settled into bed that I thoroughly wished for the technology to be able to redact my previous texts. I stayed awake late into the night wishing there was a way.

NINE

I woke up to about five texts. Pretty much all of them angry and accusatory. Pretty much all of them spot on. The one text that made no sense to me was the one where she explained that she met up with me at the designated spot at the designated time and we decided to go to the fountain in the middle of the outlet mall to conduct our experiment and how dare I accuse her of simply not showing up.

So, I called her up, ready to fight and argue about how she definitely did not show up and as soon as she answered the phone with an intense, "What?!" we both stopped for a second and realized that something had actually happened. I had suffered the same fate as all the people that are usually around when one of us dies. I didn't remember anything,. Whatever force that rendered a bit of temporary amnesia had affected me as well.

That got me to thinking about Men in Black and the little light flashy thingy they wave around. Please look into the camera and say cheese. Memory gone. Except, I wasn't given a new memory, at least I don't think I was. What if there were really humans dressed in suits and sunglasses following us around cleaning up after our deaths? Why hadn't they taken us in for testing? But then, Dolores would have seen those men, if they existed, after I was hit by the car.

"So, the event of one of our deaths triggers an event that causes a temporary amnesia episode to affect everyone who is nearby. Do you think distance has anything to do with it?" I asked, more in a musing to myself way than an actual question to Chloe.

"What do you mean by distance?" she asked.

"Well, do you think there is a radius of affectation? Outside of that radius people go on about their days none the wiser." I raised my eyebrows before remembering I was on the phone with her.

"I mean, that makes sense, because people at a certain distance wouldn't need to forget something they know nothing about."

"If that's the case, I may have found a loophole." I told her about my conversation with Dolores and Earl. How she knew for a fact that I died at the scene and my body disappeared, yet here I was at work the next day as though nothing happened.

"That's interesting. At least now we know what happens to our bodies when we die. They decompose instantly, leaving our clothes behind." I could hear Chloe clucking her tongue on the other end. She was thinking about something, and I wasn't about to interrupt her.

After a few moments, she continued, "I wonder what it looks like when we come back. Do we slowly reappear in bed? Is it like some sort of 3D printing, or is it instantaneous?"

Before I could say anything she quickly said, "Time to buy the farm, my friend."

"So, it's my turn, eh? I thought you didn't like me randomly showing up in your bed." A bit cheeky, but you have to find the joy in life somehow.

"Except I will be waiting for you this time. I will set up a video camera and everything; run it all night so we don't miss the reentry." She sounded excited. I had a sneaking suspicion she already knew how I was to die.

"So, how are you going to kill me?" I asked in an apathetic monotone.

I actually heard her clap her hands and rub them together through the phone. "That's the fun part, mon ami. I bought some steaks. I have an annual pass to the zoo."

"No." It was all I could muster.

"Lions love big ol' hunks of meat."

"Come on, Chloe. Please."

"You are going to waltz right on in there with those steaks strapped to you like C-4 and you are going to let those lions devour you."

"In front of people? You're sick."

"They won't remember. Remember?"

I nodded my head like she could see me through the phone. "I remember. It's still pretty twisted."

"Ah, yes," and in my head I saw her holding up a finger on the other end. "But it is original. I will have everything set up back in my room to await your inevitable return." She giggled.

"You are a sadist." I took a deep breath and rolled my eyes. "When do you want to send me into the lion's den?"

A slight pause and then, "You busy today?"

I seriously didn't want to do this, but fair is fair. She died yesterday, I guess I could die today. "Nooooo." I dragged the word out, hoping she would change her mind. Praying she would come to her senses.

TEN

I stared down at the animals, still wondering exactly how I made it through the front gate without being caught. The meat hung heavy from the out-of-season trench coat I was wearing, but I guess they figured there really was nothing to steal from the zoo, so they let me in, no questions asked. There were ten steaks clipped to the inside of the coat and they were starting to smell. If I was going to do this stupid thing, I better get on with it.

I counted twelve times I moved forward and stepped back before making my final decision. Everyone around me had started to cast wary glances in my direction and I was thinking some of them were starting to anticipate a stupid human trick from me. They weren't wrong.

In one swift motion I moved forward, grabbing onto the outer railing and hefting myself over toward the large chain link fence that surrounded the inner sanctum where the lions lounged, disinterestedly watching my movements.

I had scaled ten feet of the fence before anyone around me made a single noise. I think they were stunned. But by that point it was too late for anyone to do anything. With only five feet left to go I heard the voices of zookeepers under me. They were telling me to stop, or I would get hurt. And saying they wouldn't press charges if I simply came back down on this side of the fence.

As I looked down at the three zookeepers attempting to maintain some semblance of control, I flung my left foot over the top of the fence, followed by my right foot. I began my descent into the lion enclosure, suddenly unsure if this was a good idea. A cold sweat broke out on my brow and my breath came quick.

There was a moat separating the fence from the lions, and I wasn't sure exactly how I was going to pull this off. Would I be able to get enough traction to make it up the other side? There was only one way to find out, so I sat down and slid into the moat, my jacket riding up so everyone could see the steaks. I heard a collective gasp as my feet connected with the concrete at the bottom. As I made contact, I heard a small crack and my left foot exploded in agony. I couldn't put any weight on it at all. My foot had broken.

Undaunted by this turn of events I began to climb the other side of the moat, which was a lot steeper than I had originally thought. I made it about five feet before sliding back down. This was going to be impossible. I limped around the bottom of the moat, hoping to find an area that had less of a slope, but I was stuck.

I let out a roar of frustration, which was met by a roar from above me. Looking up, I saw a lion, mane blowing in the wind, staring down at me hungrily. My knees gave out. It was one thing to run with this idea of being eaten alive; it was an entirely different situation now that I was actually here in a staring contest with the king of beasts.

After what felt like an eternity the lion turned and trotted away from the edge. I didn't know what to make of the sudden shift in events, but I was both annoyed and relieved. Until I saw another head peer over the side. A human head. A human head attached to the rest of a zookeeper. It was over. I was done. This little escapade had come to an end and who knew what awaited me now that I hadn't died.

Moments later a rope was lowered, and I grabbed onto it, using my feet, mostly the one that wasn't surely broken, to propel myself upward as the zookeeper pulled on his end. I only got twisted up in the ropes once or twice and then I crested the lip of the crevasse and stood up to see three zookeepers glaring at me. One of them walked up to me and smacked me in the back of the head multiple times while saying, "Are you stupid?"

I looked away, unsure of what to say. They obviously wouldn't believe me if I mentioned that I was immortal, and I obviously had less than ideal intentions when I climbed over the fence.

The same zookeeper who knocked my brain around said, "Well, obviously you are banned from this zoo for life. We might even press charges for trespassing and reckless endangerment."

As I listened to this guy, I realized he had either *been* a cop, or had always *wanted* to be a cop. He spoke in clipped phrases to get his point across while standing straight to present his authority. And it was working. I felt bad. It was a stupid stunt, and I shouldn't have tried it. I was going to give Chloe hell for this one.

The zookeeper suddenly took on an air of paternal comfort, which made my shoulders seize up. "Let's get you out of here, huh? We can take a look at that ankle of yours, see if it's broken," he said with a tight-lipped smile on his face.

As we walked toward the zookeeper's entrance, I could hear applause behind me, and it took everything in me not to turn and take a bow. The thought *did* make me giggle a bit though. "Put the lions away, I see."

"Well, we weren't about to come in here while they were still roaming around now, were we?" the zookeeper replied.

"Smart," was all I could think to say.

As we approached their office all I could think about was how this event would be remembered going forward, because there were clearly a lot of people who saw me not die but try something crazy. I decided that after I died, I would try to come back and see if they recognized me.

In the office they bandaged my ankle and the zoo doctor informed me that it was probably broken, and I should probably go see a doctor about it. They took my picture with a Polaroid camera and tacked it to the wall where I saw pictures of a dozen other people who had been barred for life as well. I wondered if they studied those faces every morning, just in case they tried to sneak in uninvited.

After a stern lecture about zoo safety and how dangerous wild animals are and how dare I try to hurt their animals, they released me. They said next time they would press charges, because it would mean I was there after being explicitly told not to return. I nodded my head in agreement and apologized and walked back out into the sunshine.

Now what was I going to do? I needed to die for the experiment, but I was fresh out of ideas. First things first, this meat jacket had to go. It was giving me a headache and potentially ruining my future appetite for steak. Then I would figure something out. I had to. For science.

ELEVEN

I felt myself waking up and waited for the screams to begin. When they didn't, I opened one eye and scanned the room. Chloe was asleep, not manning the camera, and at first, I was angry, because it meant she didn't get me coming back. But then I saw the red light glowing and realized she had probably turned on the camera when she felt sleepy in order to not miss the event.

Even so, it was a bold move, because she could have started the tape too early and run out of space by the time I arrived. But I moved to where Chloe was sitting, asleep, slumped over with her head on her chest and checked the monitor. Numbers ticked down in the upper right corner, informing me that it was still recording.

Now, I could have been super nice and gently shook Chloe awake. Instead, I got right up next to her ear, took a lungful of air and yelled, "HOLY CRAP, I HOPE YOU GOT THAT ON TAPE!!" right in her eardrum.

The string of profanity that exited her mouth made me regret the entire thing. She mentioned something about castrating me and instead of taking it all in stride, I replied with, "It would just grow back." That was the wrong move.

I glanced at my watch to gauge how long she yelled at me, but I stopped paying attention after the seven-minute mark.

Finally, she calmed down enough to take a single gulping breath. And I seized my opportunity, hoping she would remain calm now that she had gotten it out of her system. "So, the plan had a flaw."

Chloe had opened her mouth to continue screaming at me, but this stopped her, and she begrudgingly asked, "What flaw?"

"Well, you know how at the zoo there is a gigantic moat between the fence and the actual lion enclosure? It kind of hindered my ability to even get close to the lions. I even broke my ankle. So, all in all, great success." I winked at her, hoping to get across my sarcasm and also make her laugh.

"So, how did you die?" was all she could ask.

"Boring way. Not important. What *is* important is finding out if anyone at the zoo remembers me. I'm assuming they do because of my failure, but maybe there is a general reset button for anyone who saw me at all on the day I die."

"But first—" Chloe began.

"But first, let's take a look at that video tape." I clapped my hands and rubbed them vigorously together.

Chloe grabbed the SD card out of the camera and plugged it into the side of her laptop. She spoke as she worked. "I thought I might fall asleep, so when I was getting closer, I started recording. I figured it would be about around 7am when you materialized, because I have been looking at the clock every time I come back to see if there is a pattern."

"And 7am is the pattern?" I asked, watching her open programs on her computer.

"So it would seem." She clacked a few more keys and then the footage began.

For the first few seconds there was nothing happening, and then Chloe jumped on screen and stared directly into the camera. "Is this thing on?" recorded Chloe asked. I couldn't help but laugh a bit, which earned me a backhand to the stomach.

Chloe scrubbed through the footage and stopped when she got close to the end. There was a clock in the background that read 6:55am. They waited silently for anything to happen, and after listening to recorded Chloe softly snore for a few minutes the entire visual wavered and then snapped back to clear. A few seconds after that and the screen was filled with wavy lines, making it impossible to see anything on screen. After what felt like an eternity, but was actually only twelve seconds, the screen snapped back to normal and recorded me lying on the bed.

It was over. Whatever rematerialized me had caused interference with the video feed. And Chloe had fallen asleep, so there was no in-person account of what it looked like. I slowly put my hand to my forehead and sighed. "Son of a bitch," I whispered under my breath.

"Yep," Chloe responded.

We both sat there despondent, unwilling to move. I'm fairly certain I heard Chloe sniffle once or twice, but I couldn't be sure it was her and not me.

Finally, I broke the silence. "We'll get 'em next time," I said, lamely. Chloe remained silent.

It took me a while, but I finally figured out that she was upset with herself for falling asleep and not seeing what happened when I returned. So, me, being the smooth talker I am said, "Don't worry about it. So, you fell asleep. So, the footage fritzed out when it happened. It could be worse."

Chloe wheeled on me, anger in her eyes. "Oh yeah? Worse than dying but not dying? Worse than not knowing what the hell is happening to me and why I'm different than everyone else?" Her eyes dared me to say, *except for me*, but I stayed silent. "Worse than feeling like a complete freak and not being able to talk about what is happening, because people would look at me weird?"

I continued my wise decision-making by responding, "At least we can try again, and this time you could stay awake."

Ladies and gentlemen, boys and girls, friends and foes, if you are paying close attention, you will know that me saying that was the wrong thing to do. If you are sitting up in class and taking notes, you are cringing as you read this. Your pencil just broke from trying to will me to take back what I had said. I even contemplated trying to die right then and there so this conversation would be forgotten, stricken from the record. Only one thing stopped me from doing it.

"If you die right now so I forget this conversation I will smother you with a pillow each and every time you return, for all eternity." Chloe stared straight through me.

Folks, I should have learned my lesson. I should have read my astrological fortune, because I'm fairly certain all it said for that morning was, *Keep your damn mouth shut.* But I didn't and I hadn't. Prepare yourselves, because if you were cringing before, your stomach is going to hurt now. I looked her dead in the eye and said, "But you'll forget, so it doesn't matter anyway."

The look Chloe gave me should have turned me to stone instantly. I should be a sculpture of a huddled mass of flesh, trying to disappear before her Medusa gaze. Instead, I got to take the brunt of her rage as she yelled, "If you do not leave my house this instant, I am calling the police! I will have you arrested, and they will put you in an insane asylum, because I will tell them everything about how you believe yourself to be immortal! And no matter what you say, or how much you beg or plead, they won't ever believe you! You will wither away in a padded room and when you finally die of old age you will return to this room, and I don't know if you will be young again, or you will be the world's oldest man, but I will call the cops on you again, so you repeat the cycle forever!"

Guys and gals, if you have been following this exchange as closely as I imagine you have, you know what's coming next. You have gotten an eraser out of your back pocket, and you are about to attempt to eradicate my response from this manuscript. You are readying yourself to tear this page from the book, because it hurts too much to see someone this hellbent on destroying himself. But since you *have* been involved up to this point, it will come as no surprise to you that I responded, "You'll still be living here?"

Chloe's primal scream burst my left eardrum. She looked for something to stab me with and that is when I made my exit. I had overstayed my welcome by all of it.

The only thing I could think as I walked quickly down the sidewalk away from Chloe's house, glancing over my shoulder every few seconds to make sure she wasn't following me with a knife was, *I sure can't wait until I die the next time. That'll be fun and not uncomfortable in any way at all.*

TWELVE

If aimless wanderer was a job, I would have gotten an award for being the best. I honestly had no idea where to go or what to do. Sure, I still had my job I went to, but there was nothing to fill in the gaps between. Exploring the mystery of my immortality had lost its flavor since Chloe and my giant fight. She wasn't returning my texts; I'm pretty sure she had blocked my number.

I had never been so careful in my entire life, so I didn't die and wake up on her bed. People honked at me because I would sit at an intersection an extra three seconds, to ensure no car was running a red light from the cross traffic. Avoiding crossing the street had almost become a compulsive thing. One day it took me twenty minutes to go to the little restaurant that was two blocks away.

I absolutely refused to do anything new. If I didn't know how to do it, nothing was done about it. My toilet seat cracked two days ago, and every time I sat down it pinched my butt cheek. My butt cheek was bruised from the frequent interactions. But I wasn't about to risk jamming a screwdriver through my brain by accident while changing the seat, and what if duct tape is toxic to human skin? What if I got butt cancer from too much contact with duct tape?

It had been three weeks since last I spoke with Chloe, and life was dull; lifeless. There was nothing to look forward to anymore. So, I got into a routine of watching local morning programs like *Good Morning, Cinder Falls*, going to work, coming home, watching the evening news, and falling asleep on the floor, where there was no possibility of me falling and banging my head causing an aneurysm that would lead to my death.

On this particular morning I had blended my breakfast into a super tasty smoothie of bacon, eggs, and hash browns and I sat in front of the television to watch the overly cheerful hosts of the morning talk show discuss things like how crazy it was to see the parade of dogs on skateboards yesterday at the local community center.

They had a special guest on the program, an historian who had studied the origins of Cinder Falls and what it had looked like before any settlers came to the town. I sipped my smoothie, fighting my gag reflex as my brain constantly reminded me of how I had massacred a perfectly good meal, just so I didn't choke on it…and die.

"Thank you for joining us, Dr. Hiram." Host 1 said.

"My pleasure," responded Dr. Hiram.

Host 2 leaned forward with a clever quip ready. "You look too young to be a historian."

I snorted, watching the muscles twitch on Dr. Hiram's face as he tried to maintain his composure. "Well, studying history doesn't mean I have to be a part of it. At least not yet."

Host 1, "Truer words." And that was it. She didn't say anything else.

Host 2 took up the mantle quickly enough. "So, Hiram…sorry…Dr. Hiram, tell us about what you have learned regarding our town."

Dr. Hiram took a deep breath, realizing he would have to dumb down any response so he wouldn't have to answer follow-up questions. "Well, most recently I have been intrigued by the land formations of Cinder Falls. What phenomena could have befallen this area before it was domesticated."

Host 2 grabbed him by the arm. "You mean like a housecat."

I cringed, watching Dr. Hiram's defeated expression. "Sure. Anyhow, I discovered that dinosaurs probably roamed this area millions of years ago. They did a good job of flattening the earth, making it a perfect spot for humans to settle in the future."

Host 1 looked a bit lost. "The future?"

Dr. Hiram explained, "Their future; our past."

"Of course," Host 1 said, as if he were following along perfectly.

"The dinosaurs of this region were most likely eradicated due to a meteor strike. I don't believe that is how *all* dinosaurs went extinct, but it would fit with what I have discovered over time. Tiny fragments of meteorites have been found in the dirt since ground was broken with the first people who lived here."

I leaned forward. Meteorites.

"Of course, the meteorites could have crash landed here at any point in history, but I have used the isochron method to try and date them and it seems concurrent with the extinction of the dinosaurs," Dr. Hiram continued.

Host 2 nodded his head slowly. "This isochron method sounds like a lot of work. That normal historian business, then?"

Dr. Hiram was invested in the topic despite the program he was on and tucked one leg under the other on his chair before saying, "I actually study geology as well, but it's more of a hobby. And the isochron method isn't really that difficult if you can isolate the half-life decay of rubidium-87 to strontium-87. That will give you an approximation of the age of the meteorite."

Both hosts stared at each other for a long moment, before Host 2 responded, "You know, I saw this movie once where a meteorite gave this fella superpowers. How possible is it for that to happen? If I find a large enough chunk of it, do you think I could develop the ability to fly or read minds?"

Dr. Hiram looked deflated as the realization hit him that all the morning show wanted to do was fill time. His expertise was lost in that venue. He resigned himself to the format and replied, "I highly doubt it, but if it did, I would want to have super speed."

The hosts laughed at this response, and I stopped drinking my breakfast smoothie. Could it be possible that a meteorite was behind all this? That was absurd. This wasn't a movie. But, what if? I needed to track down

Dr. Hiram and ask him some questions. Maybe as an educated man he would even believe the notion that myself and Chloe were experiencing immortal-like symptoms.

My first thought was that I needed to call Chloe and tell her about all this, but then I figured that if it turned out to be nothing at all she would be even more mad at me.

I pulled out my laptop and started a search online for how to find and contact Dr. Hiram. It didn't take long. Cinder Falls is not a big place.

THIRTEEN

Dr. Hiram maintained a lab at the community college a few miles from my house. I decided to walk the short distance. Along the way, I thought about what I could say to him to convince him that what was happening to me was real. Nothing came to mind.

I knocked on the door to LABORATORY and waited while I heard some shuffling inside. A few moments later a very flustered looking Dr. Hiram opened the door. It seemed to me that he didn't get many visitors.

I flashed my most dashing *What's up, Doc* smile and held out my hand. "Dr. Hiram, my name is Jonathan Frazier and I'm here to ask you some questions, because I cannot die." Real smooth.

He looked at my hand and then back at my face and took a step backward. "Uh huh," was all he could manage.

This was a great start to our conversation. I sighed and said, "Well, I *can* die, I am *able* to die. I just don't *stay* dead." I held up a hand in a *swear to God* motion, hoping he wasn't about to slam the door in my face.

"And I know this sounds crazy, but I saw you on the morning talk show and you were talking about meteorites, and I wanted to ask you some questions about the meteorites that landed here in Cinder Falls." I flashed another grin at the man.

He slammed the door in my face. Okay, to be more precise, he motioned like he was slamming the door in my face, but it was one of those doors with the hydraulic catch that kept it from being shut forcefully. So, we stood, staring at each other for a long moment while the door ever so slowly inched closer to separating us.

I decided to use this to my advantage. "I know I must sound crazy, Dr. Hiram, but if you allow me to explain I believe you will be able to help me with my situation."

Dr. Hiram stood still as a statue. It almost felt like he thought if he stood still enough, I would lose track of him. But I maintained eye contact and racked my brain trying to come up with something that would get me through the slowest closing door ever. The slowest closing door that, I now noticed, definitely needed its hinges oiled.

I was about to give up, when inspiration struck. "I'm not the only one. There's someone else like me. She can corroborate anything I tell you."

The door continued to close, and when it was about three inches away from the frame, Dr. Hiram's finger slipped around the door and opened it once again. He stared at me for a long while, and I tried to smile, but it felt like I had forgotten which muscles made that happen, so I stood in front of him with a grimace on my face, hoping he would say something, *anything*, to make this unbearable snapshot in time stop.

"Please come in." That's all Dr. Hiram said before he turned around and walked back to a counter that was covered with rocks and silt and a couple history books.

Silently, I followed him into the room and looked down at the rocks on the table. I saw one that was black and shiny, and I remembered something about volcanic rock forming by way of molten lava. Pointing at the shiny rock I said, "I like your basalt. It's very beautiful."

Dr. Hiram looked up at me, his brows furrowed, and as his eyes moved to see where my finger was pointing, he let out an exasperated sigh. "My dear boy, that is obsidian; an igneous rock created during the cooling process of a volcanic eruption."

I cringed. "Sorry, that's what I meant. Rocks aren't really my thing."

When I looked up at him, I could tell instantly that he was simply tolerating me at this point, so I figured I would get straight to it. "I need to know where meteorites fell or supposedly fell throughout history."

"That is a lot of data."

"I only need it for Cinder Falls. Nowhere else."

"Still a lot of data."

He was stubborn. I kind of despised him for it. "I have a specific place in Cinder Falls that I am interested in, but I don't have a topographical map to point it out."

I went to sit down, but his glare kept me standing. He walked over to a drawer and pulled out a local road atlas. He tossed it to me and simply said, "Show me."

I almost dropped the atlas but managed to snag the spiral spine between two fingertips. "Nice arm you got there," I tried to joke. No reaction. Opening the atlas, I searched for where Chloe lived, where I used to live before I burned it to the ground. It felt like hours, but had more likely been a few seconds, and I found the spot I was looking for.

Dr. Hiram snapped his fingers and reached for the atlas. I kept my finger on the spot until he had it and then he opened a journal that was filled with trace paper and overlaid one of them on top of the atlas.

There was a long silence while Dr. Hiram checked his work. "Thank you for your help," I blurted out.

"I just want you out of my lab," the curt reply came.

"I get it. I'm simply grateful you decided to help me."

Dr. Hiram made a snuffling noise through his nose.

Finally, he looked up and said, "Yep, looks like a meteorite could be somewhere very close to the location you showed me."

I felt excitement building. "So, you believe me then."

"Not a chance. In all likelihood, the meteorite is fragments of fragments. There wouldn't be enough there to even salvage. Besides the fact that meteorites do not have magical properties." He shrugged his shoulders.

"But they came from space. We don't know what kinds of properties they might possess."

Dr. Hiram deflated. "Look, kid, I'm gonna be honest with you. I believe there are meteorites that hit this area millions of years ago, but I have only found trace elements of space rocks. If I were to take my *findings* to the geological society, I would be laughed out of the building. I have a strong hunch. That's it."

I sat down heavily onto a stool. "I see." My theory had been shot down in an instant. Not that I had really expected anything more, but it was still a disappointment.

I stood up, started to stick my hand out to shake with Dr. Hiram, thought better of it, and shoved my hand into my pocket. "Sorry I wasted your time. I need to figure out why I keep coming back after I die, and I thought…" I let the thought sit in the air as I turned to leave.

The door was within my reach when I heard a defeated sigh behind me. "What did you think? That something that only happens in movies might be happening to you?"

Without turning around, I said, "Well, why not? I already keep coming back and coming back. Why not imagine that it could have to do with some meteorites?"

Another long silence, but at least I wasn't being ushered out the door quite yet. Then, "Suppose I was to believe you about coming back to life time and again. I would need you to prove it to me. And I'm sorry to say, I'm not in the position to have a dead body on my hands."

Finally, I turned to him. "That's the problem. Whenever I die, or Chloe dies, no one remembers that it happened. It's like it was erased from their memories. It even happened to me when we were trying to figure out why people couldn't remember."

I could see him mulling the thoughts over, but there was still a significant amount of doubt on his face. I tried a Hail Mary. "How about this? You come with me, and we can wait in the spot where Chloe and I reappear, and Chloe can go off somewhere else and we can demonstrate to you that we're not pulling your leg. Would that work for you?"

He shifted from one foot to the other. "Why are you telling me this? Why did you choose me? There are a hundred more qualified people in the scientific community that would be better suited to assist you in this madness."

I flashed him my brightest, most sincere smile. "Because you were the one that I saw on TV this morning. And I felt bad that you had to deal with those rabid lack-of-personalities on the program."

He nodded his head and took a deep breath. "All right, when and where do we meet?"

I grabbed a loose piece of paper and a pen and wrote down the instructions.

FOURTEEN

We had agreed to meet that evening at Chloe's house, but I still had one very large problem I had to deal with before Dr. Hiram arrived: I had to convince Chloe to give me another chance.

I got to her place in the early afternoon and parked a couple blocks away in case I was met with knives or nun chucks or a gatling. As soon as her building was in sight my palms began to sweat. Her threats still played on repeat in my head. So, I approached with extreme caution and when I had steeled myself for the task I raised my fist to knock on her door.

"What do you want?" a voice from behind me asked.

I'm not going to sugar-coat this. I screamed. It was shrill. It was the shrillest scream I had ever screamed. And it lasted a good five seconds. I tensed my body, waiting for the ending blow that would make me wake up on her bed at 7 o'clock the next morning.

When nothing happened, I turned around and Chloe was glaring at me. Maybe I was being optimistic, but her eyes seemed slightly amused despite the scowl on her face. I used it to my hopeful advantage.

"Heeeyy, buddy." Strong start. "How ya doin'?" Stronger finish.

She held up a hand, all five fingers splayed in front of her. Then she put a finger down. I got the hint.

In a rush of adrenaline and necessity I blurted out, "I think I may have a lead as to why this is all happening and the guy that I talked to is going to be here in a couple hours and I wanted to make sure that we were besties again, so maybe not besties, but…cooool…again before he got here and I looked like a fool for dragging him out here with no way to show him what I was telling him and I didn't know what…to…do."

I inhaled deeply, realizing I had said my entire piece without breathing and saw that Chloe was down to one finger left, and I will leave it to you fine detectives to figure out which finger that was.

She held the finger in front of my face for a few seconds before her whole body seemed to deflate.

"So, can we talk?" I asked, adding quickly, "Without you trying to smother me with a pillow?"

In response, she pushed past me and opened her front door. When she left it wide open I took that as my invitation to cross the threshold. I'd never been more grateful to not be a vampire.

We arrived at the bedroom and in my infinite ability to be suave and put people at ease, I patted the wall and said, "I sure did miss you. How you been?"

Chloe stared at me, a look of disgust curling her lips. "You really are an odd duck, you know that?"

Then I quacked. Might as well have had her reject me entirely or toss me in a dumpster. I felt my face grow hot.

Chloe took a seat on her bed, and I stood awkwardly by the door and started to explain what had transpired since our little falling out. To her credit, she listened intently and even nodded a couple times.

"So, he will be here at about 8pm and I figure to ensure your safety and not being left alone in your bedroom with a possible weirdo," Chloe raised her eyebrow, "another possible weirdo, you could do the experiment, and we'll wait for you to pop back onto your bed in the morning."

I gave her my cheesiest grin and did a half bow. "Thank you for coming to my TED talk."

Chloe sat with the information for a while, looking like she was alternating between wanting to kill me and wanting to solve the mystery.

In the end, the mystery won out and she said, "I don't know how you convinced Dr. Hiram to meet here, but if he can provide some answers I say we go for it." Then she added, "This doesn't make us friends, Jonathan."

I held my hands up in surrender. "Wouldn't dream of it."

A silence fell on the room, but since silences really aren't my thing, I asked, "You got anything to eat?"

At that Chloe stood up from her bed and shoved me out of the room. "Go eat at a restaurant and come back when it's time."

I offered a salute as she slammed the door in my face and went to find some food.

FIFTEEN

My belly full and my hopes slightly up, I rounded the corner heading back to Chloe's house and saw Dr. Hiram standing on the sidewalk. Not only was Dr. Hiram there, but he also had four other people with him. Confused, I walked up to him and asked, "Who are all these people?"

Dr. Hiram looked annoyed. "I figured if I was going to do this properly I would need my own crew to independently verify your claims. Video, audio, spectrometer, the works. Plus, they can place themselves in the room in such a way so that you and this girlfriend of yours can't pull any tricks."

"Not my girlfriend. Please don't refer to her as such when we get inside. If you do, she is likely to usher us all out with a knife." I tried to laugh naturally. Didn't really work.

Sighing, I led the way to Chloe's door and knocked. We stood there for a couple minutes while Chloe was most likely trying to determine if she really wanted to try this experiment. Just when I was starting to get nervous, I heard the dead bolt slide open and the door swung inward.

I thought a pre-emptive strike regarding the sudden increase in human bodies was the way to go, so I blurted out, "He brought a crew, because they want to make sure we don't make them look like idiots."

Everyone stared at me and my head swiveled from Chloe to Dr. Hiram and his crew and back. No one seemed impressed. I stepped to the side and allowed Dr. Hiram and his crew to enter before me.

Chloe pointed down the hall to her bedroom and they all moved off dutifully. I tried to enter, but Chloe stopped me with a forceful push in the chest.

"Unnecessary," I blurted.

"Don't care," she replied. "If even so much as one of my articles of clothing goes missing, I come for you first."

I blanched, a little impressed that she could intimidate me so easily still. "Sounds fair."

She stepped to the side to let me pass and I walked to her bedroom. Most of the equipment was already set up, and I noticed that Chloe had her laptop open and on the screen was the last attempt we made before our falling out.

Chloe brushed past me and whispered, "I do the talking," as she entered the room.

She walked up to Dr. Hiram and introduced herself and said, "We have the footage from the last time we tried this experiment, but of course the video fritzed out on us at the exact worst time. Which doesn't help our claim, but I still would like you to watch it and get your initial thoughts."

Dr. Hiram and his crew crowded around the laptop and Chloe pressed play. On the screen the familiar scene played out: Chloe falling asleep and then the jagged lines of the video being affected, and then I was suddenly on the bed.

The team huddled away from Chloe and myself, murmuring amongst themselves. I tried to hold my breath so I could eavesdrop, but they were very good at keeping the content to that quadrant of the room.

Finally, Dr. Hiram turned and said, "Obviously all of that could have been faked. It most likely *was* all faked. But we will make our final determination tomorrow after 7am rolls around."

For the first time I noticed two flats of energy drinks in the corner. They were not going to take the risk of falling asleep during the experiment. And for most likely the first time in my life I employed my vocal filter and kept my thoughts to myself.

There were other logistics Dr. Hiram wanted to run through, and he had a few questions as well.

"Does it matter what time of the day you die? Does that affect what time you 'come back'?" He put the last two words in air quotes.

"Nope," Chloe responded tersely. "As long as it's between the hours of 7:01am and 6:59am the next day it is always 7am when we wake up on the bed."

"And no matter where you are, you only ever wake up here, in this room?"

I barged in, I couldn't help myself. "That's why I think the meteorite might be on this site…" My voice trailed off as Chloe's glare intensified.

"That is our working hypothesis. It's the only thing that makes sense. Jonathan used to live here, and then his house burned down, the city rebuilt, and I moved in," Chloe finished.

"How long after you moved in here before you died the first time?" Dr. Hiram asked, actually seeming interested now.

"I don't know if I could pinpoint the exact amount of time, but it was at least a few weeks. So, if you're trying to determine how many sleeps one would have to have in order to gain the power, I couldn't tell you," Chloe said, answering the question she knew was coming next.

"So, technically, if we all fell asleep in this room, there is a possibility that we could all develop this power." Dr. Hiram said, and then added, "If all of this isn't some sort of magic act, of course."

"Of course," Chloe responded, a bit sardonically if you ask me. I once again managed to keep my mouth shut.

Dr. Hiram nodded his head and pulled out a tablet. He poked the screen a few times and then said, "We are going to need to search the room for any hidden ingress or egress points. We will need to watch you actually leave the premises. And, according to your boy…to your pal here, you need to make sure you are a good distance away, so we don't 'forget' what happened."

Again with the air quotes.

Chloe nodded and watched the crew looking through her room, in her closet, behind her dresser, under the bed, knocking on the floor and walls to ensure there were no false or trap doors. Lastly, Dr. Hiram grabbed hold of the handle on one of Chloe's dresser drawers and yanked it open.

"Oh, come on," I blurted out, before clapping my hand over my mouth.

Dr. Hiram turned to me, impatience shining off his body like a sick aura. "I had to make sure it wasn't hollow on the inside. Somewhere for her to stow away until the exact right moment."

"Okay," I squeaked out.

Their investigation complete, they pulled out bags of snacks and settled in for the long night. Some of them played games on their phones or laptops, one guy had a book the size of my head that he was halfway through, and Dr. Hiram stood there looking as annoyed as ever.

"Now, if you would kindly leave," he said, looking at Chloe, "I will confirm that you have left the premises and we will get on with this circus performance."

Chloe nodded her head and walked toward her front door. Dr. Hiram was close behind her and I followed them like a loyal puppy. We reached the front door, and Chloe gave me one last reproachful glance and then she was out the door and Dr. Hiram watched her walk away, and when he could no longer see her, he shut and locked the front door.

Without another word, Dr. Hiram returned to the bedroom, and I stood in the entryway, unsure if I wanted to return to hostile territory so soon.

SIXTEEN

The time was 6:40am. Somehow, no one had fallen asleep through the whole night. I had dozed a couple of times, but no one seemed concerned about me. I felt like a seventh wheel.

The energy drinks were almost all consumed, there were snack wrappers littering the floor, and since there was nothing else to do for the next twenty minutes I grabbed the garbage can and put all the wrappers in the trash, so Chloe didn't come back to a filthy bedroom.

By the time I was done the official countdown had begun. The crew was up, double checking their equipment, and slapping themselves in the face so they were prepared. Two minutes to go and I had definitely peeked at their spectrometer throughout the night and if it had done anything significant, I couldn't say.

Someone called out 30 seconds and I could feel the air being sucked out of the room. Dr. Hiram still looked unimpressed, but the rest of the crew gave off a vibe of anxious energy. There was hope in their eyes.

7am struck, and for a long moment nothing happened. There was a collective release of breath as they prepared for the anger of Dr. Hiram yelling at me, telling me I had wasted everyone's time and he would probably file a restraining order and Chloe would be mad at me and everything was garbage.

Dr. Hiram moved toward the bed a step and everyone shivered at once. The atmosphere had changed. It was as if the particles themselves had been charged up, and it was trying to find a spot to place all that energy. Dr. Hiram stopped moving and waited with bated breath.

There was no sound when Chloe reappeared. In fact, there was hardly any disturbance at all. The air was electrically charged and then all the energy rushed toward the bed and in the next instant there was Chloe. Her eyes were closed, and I moved a step closer to the bed.

I heard Dr. Hiram reverently whisper, "What the hell?" behind me, but I was focused on Chloe opening her eyes. Finally, there was a flutter and her eyes slowly opened.

The room erupted into a cacophony of inarticulate sounds and swearing, so much swearing. They all looked ecstatic and a bit shell-shocked at what they had just witnessed. I knelt by the bed and smiled at Chloe.

She looked back at me, without malice I might add, and simply said, "We did it."

I nodded and then turned to see how Dr. Hiram was reacting, but he wasn't in the room. Stepping out into the hallway I heard Dr. Hiram speaking in hushed tones.

I slowed my approach and listened closely.

"I'm telling you, I've never seen anything like it. I have eyewitnesses, and I'm sure the camera didn't capture the exact moment she reappeared, but I was here. I saw the whole thing." Dr. Hiram's excitement was palpable.

He listened for a moment and then said, "As soon as you can. We need to excavate."

Hearing those last words, I made my presence known and looked at Dr. Hiram, who held up a finger, no not that one, to indicate he would be with me shortly.

"We'll be here. See you soon," Dr. Hiram concluded and hung up the phone.

"What do you mean, an excavation?" I demanded.

"If there really is a meteorite under the ground on this spot, we need to find it," Dr. Hiram replied, a soft hysteria playing around his eyes.

"But this is where Chloe lives," I said. I couldn't believe what I was hearing.

"That's too bad." Dr. Hiram shrugged his shoulders.

Sensing impending danger, I rushed back to the bedroom and when I was nearly out of earshot I heard Dr. Hiram mumble, "It's not like she'll be living here anymore anyhow."

Ignoring the words I walked up to Chloe and took her hand. "Chloe, we have to get out of here right now. They want to destroy your house to get at the meteorite."

Chloe's face darkened and she willingly moved toward the door, still holding my hand. As we approached the hallway Dr. Hiram stepped into view, blocking our exit.

"I'm sorry, Jonathan and Chloe. I can't let you leave," he said, a hint of threat in his voice.

I tried to push past him, but he stood his ground.

"You can't do this to us," I stated firmly. "You can't make us stay."

Dr. Hiram's lips curled in a sinister manner, and he said, "The scientific community is going to be very interested in figuring out how these gifts of yours work. I've been instructed to keep you on premises until the proper authorities can transport you to your new living quarters."

I stepped up and pointed a finger in his face and said, "Listen up you cliched super villain bastard, we have rights. You can't just hush this up."

Dr. Hiram leaned in really close, like far too close, like I could have kissed his nose by extending my lips the slightest bit. I mean, I didn't, but I could have. That's the point I'm trying to make. But he smiled in my face and it was very reminiscent of the Grinch.

"Oh, but we absolutely can and will. So, you might as well have a seat and wait this one out quietly." And with a quick flick of his eyes, he motioned for a couple of his men to restrain us.

We were pushed onto the bed next to each other and Chloe let go of my hand. "I hate you!" she said through clenched teeth.

I nodded. "Yeah, I kind of hate me too."

And then we lapsed into silence until there was a knock at the door.

SEVENTEEN

They told me I could write all of this down. As much as my little heart desired. Because, in their words, no one would ever believe me anyhow. So, I have been writing down my story as best I can recall. Sure, I might have made myself look better, more the hero than I am, but I wanted to be honest with my retelling.

Chloe and I are kept in separate rooms. They're cozy enough, and I never have to worry about my next meal, but we are not allowed to leave under any circumstance.

After our last experiment with Dr. Hiram they tore down Chloe's building and within the week had located a large chunk of meteorite that was nestled snugly fifty feet beneath the surface. In order to conduct their own experiments in a closed environment, they moved the chunk to their facility. It's actually across the hall from me. And every evening they take blood from Chloe and myself and then make us die and wait for us to appear in the Meteorite Room and then take more blood samples. I hope they find what they're looking for, so we can move on with our lives. But, it feels like we might be here a while.

Chloe spent the first month livid every single day. They had their safe-guards to make sure we didn't kill ourselves before they had transported the meteorite on-site. Restraints at night, no shoelaces, no sharp objects, the inability to create a puddle of liquid more than an inch deep. We were constantly monitored and attended to. Once the meteorite was snug in its room they didn't care anymore. What could we do? Nothing, that's what.

One thing, I get hit a lot when we wake up in the M.R. That's what I call the Meteorite Room. Sometimes it feels like the guards wait a little longer than entirely necessary to separate us.

So, here we stay, our rights stripped away. We are essentially a black op at this point. I believe they refer to where we are as a black site.

But I will continue to write and hopefully one day I'll get a book deal. Hey, a boy can dream.

843

This morning when I woke up I braced myself for more hitting, squeezing my eyes shut, anticipating the pain. But none came. Slowly, I opened my eyes and peeked at where Chloe usually appeared. She seemed to be mesmerized by something, so I propped myself up on my elbows and looked past her to see what fascinated her so much. It would seem that we have someone new to get to know.

ACKNOWLEDGEMENTS

I hope you enjoyed the stories I have written and confined within these pages. If you didn't, I hope you find other stories that spark your imagination. Either way, thank you for taking a chance on me.

As always, I have to thank my wife for her non-stop encouragement and willingness to let me spew random thoughts at her to help my stories make enough sense to write them coherently. She never shies away from pointing out flaws in my ideas or adding her own thoughts into the mix. Without her I don't believe I would have come this far in my book writing journey.

Thank you to my Beta readers. I added a few more this time around and if I forget you, please don't be mad at me. This old brain sometimes forgets it's supposed to remember things. To the dual Pauls, the two Sams, Chad, Trevor, and Megan, I appreciate all the input you all provide to me. It is invaluable and encouraging. To Paul, my dad, who edits all my work, thank you so much for continuing to read through my wacky ideas and help fix errors and incongruities so people can enjoy my stories without getting confused. To my ARC readers, this is the first time I have actually had ARC readers and I am so grateful there are people out there who love to do that sort of work.

And, as always, thank you to those of you who choose to read what comes out of my twisted brain. You are amazing!

www.ingramcontent.com/pod-product-compliance
Lightning Source LLC
Chambersburg PA
CBHW032250310726